for Kassandra,
with love.

your uncle
april 10, 2004

MUSTAFA MUTABARUKA

Akashic Books
New York

This is a work of fiction. All names, characters, places, and incidents are the product of the author's imagination. Any resemblance to real events or persons, living or dead, is entirely coincidental.

Published by Akashic Books
©2002 Mustafa Mutabaruka

Cover photograph by Unknown

ISBN: 1-888451-31-9
Library of Congress Control Number: 2002101545
All rights reserved
First printing
Printed in Canada

Akashic Books
PO Box 1456
New York, NY 10009
Akashic7@aol.com
www.akashicbooks.com

The song lyrics, *'You can think of a whole lot of good stuff to tell a nigger when you're—'* which appear on pages 3 and 176, are quoted from 'The Rap' by Millie Jackson. The line, *'They'll never stay home, and they're always alone, even with someone they love,'* is excerpted on page 7 from 'Mamas, Don't Let Your Babies Grow Up to be Cowboys' by Ed & Patsy Bruce.

For delphine, the second most beautiful of seven sisters; and for my mother, the first.

I want to help you. I want to comfort you, but I know I disgust you. I'm repulsive to you. And I know it because you disgust me. When slaves love one another, it's not love.

—from *The Maids* by Jean Genet

'You can stop now.'

I open my eyes.

'What?'

'You can stop shaking your head,' she says, 'and pass me my purse.'

I lean forward, picking her small, red-sequined purse off the floor, and pass it to her. She takes it, opens it, and begins rummaging through the jumbled contents. Unable to find what she is looking for, she turns the purse upside down and spills its contents onto the bed.

'Here we go,' she says. 'Watch this.'

She picks up a safety pin, bends, then straightens it, and looks at me.

'Open your eyes,' she demands.

'They are open,' I reply.

'Oh, God,' she says, groaning. 'You're pathetic. Really, you are.'

I shrug.

She looks at me and frowns.

'Anyway,' she says, rolling her eyes, 'just stay with me, okay?'

Again, I shrug.

'Okay?'
'Okay,' I reply.

I watch as she raises the safety pin and, opening her mouth as if to show me what is inside, pushes its tip through her cheek. Raising her left hand, she puts her index finger inside her mouth and, with her thumb, snaps the safety pin shut.

'See,' she says, the pin's rounded tip hanging over her bottom lip. 'No blood. No pain.'

I say nothing, watching her; I am beginning to get an erection.

She unsnaps the safety pin, then pulls it, as if a sliver, out of her cheek. Gently tapping the smooth, unblemished skin with her middle finger, she tosses the pin onto the bed and smiles at me.

'You should see how people react,' she says, 'when I do it in a bar.'

I lower my hand, squeezing my erection through my trousers.

'This turns you on?' she asks, raising her eyebrows.

'You turn me on,' I reply.

'I'm sure I do,' she says, beginning to pick up her belongings from the bed and return them to her purse. Once done, she retrieves a small, silver tube, unscrews its lid, and applies a thick layer of dark red lipstick. Finished, she drops the tube into her purse, then sets it next to the bed.

'Does this turn you on?' she asks, giggling.

'Its possibilities do,' I reply, unbuttoning my trousers.

Unsteady, I step back, resting against the wall, and slowly undo the remaining buttons.

'Did your father have a big dick?' she asks.

'No,' I reply. 'But my son does.'

'Your son?'

'Yeah,' I reply. 'My son. Ulysses.'

She looks at me and smiles, then leans forward and slowly crawls, on her hands and knees, to the end of the bed.

'Tell me all about him,' she whispers.

I turn and walk slowly to the end of the hallway. If I think of anything, it is of the need to think nothing, aware of only that which is before me: the dark red walls, the wooden floor, my movement past, upon.

My grandfather's bedroom door is open; passing, I glance inside the small, windowless room, but I do not stop.

At the end of the hallway, I stand before my father's bedroom and slowly open the door. He is on the bed beneath the window, his naked body stretched out in the dim, early-evening light. The room is warm and small, shadow overlapping shadow, with a bed, dresser, and desk. I step through the narrow doorway and walk to the bed.

His hands are at his side, legs together, his face tilted up and to the left, as if, upon death, he had been looking out the window. His eyes are closed, as is his mouth, and on his left cheek, just below the eye, is a single drop of blood. I look up at the ceiling, then down; across his feet is a dark red blanket.

His body is nearly hairless. He is a big man, tall and broad, muscular, with huge, worn hands and feet. Like me, he is uncircumcised. His cock is big, I think, but his balls are small, like a young boy's or a bodybuilder's, and briefly I am embarrassed. I raise my head and look out the window into the clear, dark sky.

I close my eyes, whispering:

'You can think of a whole lot of good stuff to tell a nigger when you're—'

I open my eyes and reach for the edge of the dull gray bed sheet on which he lay. I pull it up and over him, then walk around to the opposite side of the bed and do the same. I wrap him with the thin sheet, as if in a cocoon, then knot its ends. I do this as if I have done it before.

I move quickly and lift him up, over my shoulder, holding his legs with both of my arms. Staring down at the wooden floor, I step forward, and say:

'One.'

Though not as heavy as I had imagined, his limbs are stiff, awkward, and I stumble with the body out of the room, down the narrow stairway, through the kitchen, and out of the house.

'Thirty-one, thirty-two,' I whisper, 'thirty-three, thirty-four, thirty-five.'

I move slowly across the yard and through the trees, staring at the ground as I walk.

'Fifty-two, fifty-three, fifty-four.'

The path through the trees is narrow and sloping, winding; I move with caution.

'Eighty-nine, ninety, ninety-one, ninety-two.'

Reaching the empty grave, I take a final step.

'One hundred and seventeen.'

Kneeling, I lean forward, then lie the body by the side of the grave. I stand. Breathing deeply, slowly, I rest my hands on my hips and look around.

From deep in the shadows that rise up around the small clearing, I hear the quick, lone hoot of an owl. Above me, the sky is clear and dark, darkening. I am tempted, briefly, to return to the house for a lantern. I do not.

I kneel again, take the end of the sheet, and slowly, carefully, lower my father into his grave. Satisfied with the body's position, I stand, grab the shovel, and begin to fill the shallow grave with dirt. I move quickly, thoughtlessly.

I work nonstop until I am done. I am done sooner than I had expected. An hour, two hours, three? Twenty minutes? I do not know.

I drop the shovel at my side and look into the darkness. I am sweating, trembling. Across my back, from shoulder to shoulder, is a sharp pain. My left hand, between the thumb and forefinger, is raw, bleeding.

Like a door opening, then abruptly closing, a thought begins to form and, just as quickly, fade. Staring into the trees, I whisper:

'She belonged to you. Watch.'

Turning, I step away from the grave and walk through the trees to the river. I take off my boots and undress. I fold my clothes and place them neatly in a pile next to my boots.

Naked, I step slowly into the cool, black, slow-flowing water and swim to its center. A breeze flutters across the surface, causing me to shiver, as I look up into the night, close my eyes, and let myself sink.

The first bullet misses her. As she scrambles to her feet, the second hits her in the jaw and she is thrown, by its force, to the ground. I close my eyes. My father grabs me by the neck and says, calmly:

'She belonged to you. Watch.'

I move through the house, looking, touching. I have lived much of my life in this house, but now it is different; it is foreign. I open boxes and cupboards and closets. I look through albums and letters and trunks of old clothes. If I am looking for something, anything, I do not find it.

Soon, I am bored.

It is a big house, bigger than I remember, old and cluttered, with narrow hallways, stairways, and wooden floors. Surrounded by trees, the many windows offer little light or fresh air, and the rooms are dark, musty. It is what it is, I think: an old, two-story farmhouse in which the owner has recently died.

I stand in the bedroom of my youth, looking at the books that line the shelves; there are hundreds of them. Fiction, non-fiction, hardbacked, softbacked, art books, reference books, schoolbooks.

'Meaningless,' my father often said. 'Every last one of them.'

At the time, as a young man, I had been hurt by his disregard, angered by it, but much later I came to wonder if, perhaps, he was correct.

Did it, all of it, mean nothing?

I told him, long before he died, that I would one day write about him. I meant it as a threat, of course, as a promise that I would show the world what kind of man, what kind of father, he was.

'Do you think anybody will care?' he had asked, smiling. 'And even if they do,' he added, 'what will it matter? What will it change?'

It was a question, as with all his questions, I was not expected to answer. We would still, always, if I ever wrote of him, be father and son. Perhaps I would feel better and he worse, or I worse and he better, but, alas, as he often said, the world would keep spinning as it always had and always would.

'Nothing will change,' he liked to say, 'because nothing *can* change.'

I look out the window and again to the books.

'You are not the first son,' he once said, 'to write of your father. Nor will you be the last. The fact, even, that you are inspired to write about me—that you are inspired to write, period—is proof of your pedestrian nature. Proof that your desire to write, to create, is as acquiescent to the laws of nature as what you create.'

'Sprout wings and fly,' he told me, 'and then I'll be impressed. Or better yet,' he added, 'be quiet.'

Otherwise, he believed, there was nothing a man could do, say, think, or create that would in any which way disrupt the inevitability of life—and our role within it.

'We are products,' he explained, 'not producers.'

I turn from the books and leave the room. I stand in the narrow, darkened hallway and look to my left. Next to my room is my grandfather's room, empty, unused for years. At the end of the hallway, closed, is the door to my father's room.

'Tell me something I don't know,' he liked to say. 'Show me something I have yet to see.'

I walk to the door, open it, and look inside. It is as I last left it: dark and warm, the mattress bare. On the wall above the bed is a painting of six dogs playing poker.

I walk to the bed, sit down, and look out the window. The sky is clear and bright.

'If Jesus was unable to enlighten us,' he once asked, 'what makes you think *you* can?'

'No,' I had wanted to ask, 'what makes you think *you* can?'

I turn, looking down at the dusty, wooden floor. I am the only son of an only son, I think. And I am the father of—I shrug, as if in reply, then walk out of the room, down the stairs, and out of the house.

I stand beneath the shade of the verandah and look through the trees to the barn and, further, to the lush, rolling field that stretches into the distance. I turn, scanning the yard, tracing its periphery to the mouth of the path that leads first to his grave, then to the river.

I am restless.

I step back into the house. I look around the kitchen; it is cluttered, gloomy. I walk to the cupboard above the sink, open it, and retrieve an unopened bottle of bourbon. I turn, resting against the sink, and unscrew its cap; I take one gulp, then another.

'They'll never stay home,' I whisper, 'and they're always alone, even with someone they love.'

Again, I take a gulp of the bourbon.

'If Jesus was unable to enlighten us,' he asks, 'what makes you think *you* can?'

I look at him; he is smiling. In his hand is a copy of my recently published book of poetry. I think for a moment, then reply, simply:

'I don't know.'

He leans forward, resting the book on the table between us.

'You don't know,' he says, 'because you don't want to know.'

He sits back in the chair and folds his arms across his chest.

'Because if the truth is as important to you as—'

He pauses.

'As you poets say it is,' he continues, 'you would never, none of you, write another word.'

I look at him as he looks at me. He is no longer smiling.

'Words are symbols,' he says, 'of what we see and feel. And, like all artists, like all people, you confuse, cheapen, both the symbol and its reality with—'

He holds up the book.

'With your attempt here to manipulate both.'

'Jesus did enlighten us,' I reply. 'So did the poets and artists and all of—'

'Prove it,' he interrupts. 'Look at the world in which we live and prove to me that we are enlightened. That we, humanity, are any kinder or smarter or in any way better because of Jesus. Because of Shakespeare or Tolstoy or Muhammad or, even, John Coltrane.'

'Go ahead,' he challenges. 'Prove it.'

'We are no longer slaves,' I say.

'Perhaps,' he smiles. 'But someone, somewhere, is. And always will be. And if all these thousands of years of evolution, of art and poetry and philosophy and music, have yet to change even that, nothing ever will.'

'I don't agree with you,' I say.

'Because you're weak,' he replies, 'Because you're weak and you're stupid. Like all men.'

I look at him.

'Like you?' I ask.

'Like me,' he smiles, and we sit there, then, in the shadowed warmth of the kitchen, looking at one another.

Outside, the dog barks.

I open my eyes and peer into the darkness. I am on the living room sofa, shirtless. Between my legs is the bottle of bourbon.

What time is it? I wonder. Midnight?

Through the silhouette of the trees outside the living room window, I see the distant, yellow glow of the light above the barn door.

I sit up, take the bottle from between my legs, and set it next to the sofa. My mouth is dry, sour. From the kitchen, I hear the low, heavy hum of the refrigerator.

I am not a poet, I think. I am a dancer.

I am tempted, momentarily, to stand, grab my shirt, walk out of the house, get in my truck, and drive to the airport. My flight, I know, does not leave until tomorrow, but I would rather be there, I think, in the airport, than here.

There is the future; here is the past.

I step slowly through the dark, and turn on the overhead light. I look at the mess of boxes before me, then turn, walk into the kitchen, and switch on the light above the stove. I stand, motionless, and look at the clock on the wall. It is just past midnight. I return to the living room, pick up the bottle of bourbon, take a swig, and go upstairs.

In the bathroom, I set the bottle on the top of the toilet tank and undress. Naked, I sit on the toilet, then turn and grab the bourbon. I take a sip and look at the pale, blue-tiled floor. It is clean, I think, and I am surprised.

Once done, I flush the toilet and turn to the mirror above the sink. Again, I set the bottle on the tank and look at my reflection.

I raise my hand to the mirror, gently touching its cool surface with my fingertips.

'Permanus Lucien Dove,' I whisper, staring at my reflection, 'begat Toussaint Marcus Dove. Toussaint Marcus Dove begat—'

I stop.

'Begat—?'

I move my index finger across the mirror, slowly tracing my reflection.

'Shit,' I whisper.

I lower my hand, staring at my reflection.

I am exactly six feet tall and I weigh one hundred and ninety pounds. My father was six feet and one inch tall. He weighed, I imagine, close to two hundred and fifty pounds, all muscle. Like him, I am nearly hairless.

From my cock to my belly button, forming a trail through the pubic hair, is a thick, smooth scar. Delicately, I run my thumb along its raised surface, slowly tracing its length.

'The measure of a man,' my father once said, 'is in his scars. Without a scar, he isn't even a man. He is, merely, male.'

Cupping my balls, I lean forward, raising them, and look at the small, crescent-shaped keloid on my left testicle. I pinch the loose folds of my scrotum between my thumb and forefinger, feeling the hardened tissue, then stand straight.

I lean toward the mirror, thinking: Sometimes I look so dark, then other times so pale. I raise my head, turning to the left, then to the right, and think: But I don't even look like him. Not really. I am dark like him, if lighter, with the features, I am told, of the Cree Indian.

'Like your mother,' he once said.

I step back from the mirror. I stare at my reflection, not moving. I reach for the razor that rests on the sink's edge and quickly, though the blade is dull, cut off my left nipple.

I am not as big as him, I think; I am bigger.

Naked, he sits on the edge of the empty bathtub and stares at the pale, blue-tiled floor. His penis is erect, huge, rising up like a fist against his belly. What, I wonder, is he doing?

I shift my position, holding a branch for support, and, through the window, I watch him. Still, he does not move.

His penis both fascinates and frightens me. Other than my own, at seven, I have never seen one before. It is huge, awful, and I cannot look away.

Suddenly, he looks up. Frightened that he will see me, has already seen me, I close my eyes. I wait, silently counting to thirty, then open them; again, he is looking at the floor.

His hands are at his side, shoulders slumped, as if tired, and his legs just inches apart. His erection, I see, is becoming soft, curving forward slowly, steadily, until it rests, finally, between his thighs.

I watch him as he continues to sit, not moving, then I turn and slowly climb down the tree.

It is windy outside and the tree branches tap lightly against the windowpane. I am in the bathtub, staring at the water as it drips slowly from the rusted tap. I raise my head and, turning around, look out the window into the darkness. Through the branches, I see the half-moon, the stars; I look for a moment, then abruptly look away.

On the edge of the tub, near my feet, is the bottle of bourbon. I look at it, then whisper:

'Drink it.'

Leaning forward, I grab the half-empty bottle, holding it to my mouth. Abruptly, I lower the bottle, setting it on the floor beside me.

'But I'm not thirsty,' I say.

I stand and step out of the tub. I dry myself with a towel and, when done, drape it over the rack. I stare at my reflection in the mirror and touch the wound on my chest.

Why did I do it? I wonder.

'Understanding your desire,' my father once said, 'sometimes destroys it.'

'Other times,' he added, 'it merely increases it.'

I have cut myself, I think, raising my hand to my chest and resting it firmly over the wound, because I can.

'Drink it,' he says.

'But I'm not thirsty,' I reply.

He bends forward and, just inches from my face, whispers:

'You poured it; now drink it.'

I step back, frightened.

'I poured too much,' I say.

'What were you going to do with the rest, then?'

'Save it for later.'

He stands straight and looks down at me. He picks up the glass of milk from the table and holds it in front of my face. His hands are huge and dark; they smell of gasoline.

'You do this all the time; you pour a full glass of milk and then you drink only half. The rest you pour in the sink.'

'No I don't.'
'Yes you do.'
His voice is calm.
'Drink it,' he says.
'I can't.'
He smacks me across the face, then again, knocking me off balance. I begin to cry.
'Why are you crying?' he asks.
'Because you hit me,' I reply.
He hits me again.
'You're seven years old,' he says. 'Act like it.'
I say nothing, continuing to cry.
'Now, are you going to drink it?'
I reach for the glass of milk and, taking it from his hand, I drink it. Finished, I hold up the empty glass, expecting him to take it; he does not. I place it on the kitchen table and turn, as if to leave.
'You're not done,' he says.
I turn back, looking at the empty glass, then at his hands; they are at his side.
'What do you mean?' I ask. 'I—I drank it all.'
'No you didn't. I want you to drink it all.'
I look again at the glass, but it is, indeed, empty. I do not know what to say.
'Dad,' I say. 'It's all gone. I drank it all.'
He reaches forward, grabbing me by the back of the neck, and forces me toward the counter. There, at eye level, next to the sink, is the jug of milk; it is nearly full.
'No,' he says. 'You didn't.'
I look up at him and say:
'Dad, I can't drink that.'
Abruptly, he bangs my head against the side of the counter, then pushes me to the floor. Everything, suddenly, is a blur. I sit, not moving; he grabs me by the shoulder and lifts me to my feet. He shoves me toward the table and screams:

'Sit down!'

I sit on one of the chairs, still crying, and watch as he takes the glass jug of milk and places it on the table in front of me.

'And I'll tell you right now, nigger, you better stop that crying. Do you hear me? You want to be a man, then you start acting like one. Now, drink.'

He opens the jug of milk and fills the glass.

'Drink.'

I drink.

'Don't stop,' he says softly. 'Keep drinking.'

I look at his hands.

I finish the glass of milk; he pours another. I finish it; he pours another. I throw up. I drink half of the glass and then, again, throw up.

He does not move; he stands and he watches.

'Keep drinking,' he says. 'You'll clean up this mess when you're done.'

I keep drinking.

'A baby,' he says. 'Seven years old and still acting like a baby.'

I drink another glass, then another; I throw up. I drink half of a glass and, again, throw up; the vomit is pink and he tells me to stop.

'Clean this up and then go to bed,' he says. 'You can drink the rest tomorrow.'

The house is quiet.

I sit up, slowly, putting my feet on the floor, and look into the shadows. I am about to stand when, suddenly, I hear the kitchen door open, then close.

My body tenses, but I do not move.

I hear the sound of bare, wet feet walking across the wooden floor. The steps are heavy, plodding. I peer into the darkness of the kitchen and, I am certain, see a shadow move slowly in front of the window. I close my eyes.

There is silence.

I sit, completely still, then open my eyes. In an instant, I relax, then shake my head. I look into the darkness and say:

'Fuck me.'

I take a deep breath and lean forward, resting my elbows on my thighs. I shiver, briefly, then smile; I am both relieved and embarrassed.

'Fuck me,' I say again.

I stand, walk into the kitchen, turn on the light, and glance at the floor. There are no footprints and, briefly, I am disappointed. I walk to the sink and look out the window; it will soon be dawn.

I move from the window and walk out the door onto the verandah. I stare into the early morning darkness. The sun is beginning to rise, and the sky, in the distance, is a sliver of pale blue, orange, pink. The morning air, though slightly humid, is cool.

I turn and step back into the house. I look at the clock; it is 4:47 a.m. Quickly, I begin to clean, to organize. I fill boxes, then stack the boxes. I stack and line and dust and sweep. I mop.

The sun rises, has risen, and I continue: from the kitchen to the living room to the storage room to the bedrooms and bathroom. I open the cellar door but, just as quickly, close it.

'You'll clean up this mess when you're done,' I say.

I make a pot of coffee; I drink four cups, one after the other. I eat a banana. I return to each room in the house; the floors are clean, beds are made, were already made, everything folded and organized and neat and closed and wiped. It has taken me, perhaps, four hours, and I am finished; there is nothing left to do.

I put on a shirt, socks, my shoes, move my suitcase downstairs to the kitchen, and sit. I look out the window, then at the table before me. In its center, I notice, is my plane ticket. I feel a hand on my shoulder and, without moving, I say:

'That's funny, I was just thinking about you.'

'I imagined you dead,' I say.

He looks at me and smiles, saying nothing.

'I imagined burying you,' I continue. 'I imagined a warm summer night and I carried you through the woods and I buried you in a grave and I felt nothing, not even relief. I even imagined hearing you return from your grave and walk across the kitchen floor and imagined then that it was all my imagination. God.'

What are you thinking? I want to ask. Instead, I remain silent for a moment, looking at him, then continue speaking.

'How can I explain that I wanted you dead, imagined it, but imagining it, I imagined not caring? I don't know. I can't explain it. I always—you know, I always, well, there were many times I imagined you dead. Wished you dead. And sometimes I was happy, and sometimes I was sad, and this time I didn't care. I saw myself sitting and thinking and not caring and wondering, even, if I was just pretending not to care. Just—well, I'm not making any sense, am I? Of course I'm not.'

He unfolds his arms and leans forward, clasping his hands and resting them on the table. He looks at me; he has not stopped looking at me. Still, he smiles.

'Ulysses,' he says, 'what do you want me to say? Do you want me to make you feel better? Ease your guilt? What? Do you want me to tell you it's normal to wish your father dead? To think about him in—'

He abruptly pauses, frowning.

'Son,' he says, 'your nose is bleeding.'

I raise my hand, touching my upper lip. It is wet with blood; I look at my fingertips, then at my father. He stares at me as if he is repulsed; ashamed, I look away, wiping the blood with the back of my hand.

Suddenly, I feel something smooth and solid begin to slide down, and out of, my nasal passage. As if to stop it, I put my thumb and forefinger, again, to my nose.

'Dad,' I say, then become silent.

I begin to pull the bloodied mass, long and slick, like a worm, from my nostril. It is the color, and texture, I think, of liver. Terrified, I look up at my father.

He stares at me, angry, then stands, his chair falling back to the floor, and says:

'Ulysses, what is—what?'

Blood begins to gush from my nose, thick and clotted, almost black, as I continue to pull at the—viscous, it sticks, like mucus, to my fingers as I lean forward, dazed, horrified. The room begins to shift, then spin. I hear my father, as if from another room, calling my name as he moves to my side, putting his hands to my head and pulling me back in the chair.

'Dad!' I scream, looking up into his huge, dark, blank face. 'Dad, don't—'

'What have you been doing?' he asks.

I hold the bar of soap and look at it.

'Dad,' he says, 'I don't understand what—listen, I can't help you if you don't tell me what's wrong.'

His voice is patient, condescending, and I wish he would leave.

'I can bathe myself,' I say, staring at the bar of soap.

'No,' he replies, 'you can't.'

He takes the soap from my hand, dips it in the water, and begins to lather my back and shoulders.

'Either there's nothing wrong with you,' he says, 'or it's worse than I thought.'

He pushes me forward and continues to roughly wash my back.

'I just don't understand it,' he says. 'I'm gone overnight and—and I come back to find you've cleaned the entire house and packed your suitcase as if—Dad, and, my God, cut your nipple off!'

He rinses my back and shoulders with the bath water.

'Talk to me, Dad,' he says, gently pushing me backward, where I rest, then, against the tub.

'I can bathe myself,' I say, ignoring his questions.

He rests his elbows on the edge of the tub, the soap in his hands, and looks at me.

'Well,' he says, 'I guess if you can clean the entire house, you can, indeed, bathe yourself.'

He hands me the bar of soap, and I take it from him. I look at him as he stands, then sits on the toilet, watching me.

'Go ahead, then,' he says.

'I don't need you to watch me,' I say.

'Yes,' he replies, 'you do.'

He folds his arms and I am reminded of an impatient grade school teacher. I look down at the bar of blue soap in my hand and let it fall into the bath water. He leans forward, sliding off the toilet, kneels next to the tub, and grabs the soap.

'Jesus, Dad,' he says. 'Make up your mind.'

I do not move as he begins to quickly, but gently, wash my entire body. He says nothing as he does this, moving my limbs, guiding them, scrubbing them, rinsing them. I wonder if he will wash between my legs; he does, pulling back my foreskin, even. Once finished, he pulls the plug, helps me out of the tub, and dries me with a towel. I stand, listening to the water drain from the tub.

'Dad,' he says, 'you know I want to help you. But you have to be honest with me. You have to—oh, Lord. I just don't know what's happening. I don't.'

He stands straight, draping the towel over the edge of the tub, and takes my forearm, guiding me out of the bathroom and down the hallway to my bedroom. He sits me on the bed and rubs lotion on my scalp and arms and legs. He dresses me in a pair of brown corduroy trousers, a white, short-sleeved shirt, and the soft, black-leather bedroom slippers I have worn for years.

'There,' he says, standing before me. 'Is that okay?'

We look at each other.

'A dancer,' I say. 'Are you a dancer?'

'Dad,' he replies, frowning sadly, 'yes, I'm a dancer. You know I'm a dancer.'

He kneels before me and puts his hands on my knees. He looks up at me, staring into my eyes.

'Dad,' he asks, 'do you know who I am? Do you?'

'You're a dancer,' I reply.

'Yes,' he says, 'and I'm your son; do you know my name?'

'Ulysses,' I reply.

He nods, smiling softly, and asks:

'And what is your name?'

'I'm not crazy,' I say. 'So don't talk to me like I am, damnit.'

He closes his eyes, exhaling, as if exhausted, then opens them and slowly shakes his head.

'Then why do you act like you are?' he asks, standing.

He is tall and muscular, dark, handsome, more like his mother than like me. Too big, I think, to be a dancer. But that is just what he is: a dancer.

'Because it pleases you,' I reply.

'No, Dad,' he says, as if disgusted. 'It doesn't.'

Yes, it does, I think. You just don't know it.

He stands, then sits on the bed next to me.

'Dad,' he says, 'are you conscious of doing these things? I mean, when you do them, do you know you're doing them?'

'Do what?' I ask, knowing that the question will irritate him.

'Dad!' he exclaims. 'Do—God, cleaning the house, cutting yourself, walking out into the woods at one in the morning, not moving for days, then not sitting still, not sleeping, calling me names I don't recognize, calling me *Dad*, pacing the hallway, Christ, for hours, and then forgetting, or pretending to forget, and—and just all this crazy behavior.'

I look out the window and say nothing.

'I know you're sick,' he continues, 'but I don't understand how—how it's affecting your mind. And I hope I'm wrong, but sometimes I just, well, I really think sometimes you're just doing it to irritate me, to test me. And if you are, why? But if you're not, then I want to know if you're conscious of it when it's happening. Tell me, Dad, are you?'

Still, I say nothing.

'Well,' he says, 'whatever's happening is—God, I just don't

know. I can't understand it. And maybe I don't want to. I guess. I guess I just don't know.'

'You're repeating yourself,' I say.

He looks at me and frowns.

'Well,' he says, 'that much is the same; you're still a—'

He stops.

He turns and glances out the door into the hallway.

'Do you want to go sit on the verandah?' he asks. 'Or in the living room?'

'The verandah,' I reply.

'Are you walking?' he asks, and I hear the sarcasm in his voice. 'Or do you need my help?'

I say nothing, standing, and walk slowly out of the room. He does not follow me.

I sit on the bench beneath the shade of the verandah, my hands on my knees, and stare out into the yard. The day is hot and windy, and the sun is bright. It has been weeks since the lawn was mowed, and its grass is long and littered with dandelions.

'I am not crazy,' I whisper, watching as an orange and black butterfly lands on the verandah's railing, flutters its wings, then flies away.

I hear Ulysses in the kitchen, sliding a chair across the floor and, I assume, sitting down. Last week, I remember, he threatened to return me to the hospital.

'I am a full-grown man,' I said. 'I can take care of myself.'

'You're an old man,' he replied. 'And you're sick, and you're all alone on this farm. And, no, you cannot take care of yourself.'

He does not want to be here, I know, any more than I want him to be here.

'How do I take care of you,' he often says, 'when I don't know what's wrong with you, when even the doctors don't know what's wrong?'

He believes my sickness to be psychological; I am, he says, simply willing myself, in his words, to disintegrate. I tell him this is not true, but he does not believe me. He just looks at me and shakes his head.

If I could will myself to die, I want to tell him, I would already be dead.

'A dancer,' he says. 'Of all the useless, fucking things to be, good Lord, he's a dancer. A dancer. I bet he's queer, too.'

'My son isn't queer. Not all dancers are queer, Dad.'

'Well,' he says, 'being a queer or a—a ballerina—it's all the same fucking thing. Useless. Just like you and your writing.'

'He's not a ballerina,' I say. 'He's a dancer. He dances. And my writing wasn't—'

'Oh, a ballerina doesn't dance?' he mocks, interrupting me. 'A ballerina isn't a dancer?'

A ballerina is a dancer, I want to say. But a dancer isn't necessarily a ballerina. Instead, I shake my head and look out the window.

Why, I wonder, do I talk to him? If he was stupid, I think, I could, perhaps, reason with him, *convince* him, but he is not. He is a self-educated man, well-read, and, as such, his ignorance is fundamental, innate. *He will not be moved.*

Upstairs, I hear Ulysses walking across his bedroom floor, and I wonder, briefly, if he has heard us talking. But what does it matter? I tell myself; it's nothing he hasn't heard before.

I turn and look at my father. He has fallen asleep and I am struck, watching him, by how old and frail he looks. Just an old, bitter man, I think, asleep at the kitchen table.

I look up at the ceiling and listen to the sound of my son's footsteps. And when I look at Ulysses, I reflect, I am struck by his youth. Jealous, even, of his energy and strength and bright, black eyes. Jealous, too, of his ignorance.

He reminds me of his mother. As I, I've been told, reminded my father of mine. And is it this presence, this *memory*, I briefly wonder, that keeps a man from killing his son? I smile at such a thought and turn, again, to my father. He is softly snoring, and

I slam my fist onto the table. He is startled from his sleep, mouth open, and he looks at me, angry.

'What the hell?' he says.

'Dad,' I say, 'go to bed if you're tired.'

I open my eyes. The sun has begun to set, and I think, good Lord, did I fall asleep?

I look to the driveway; Ulysses's dark red Ford pickup truck is no longer there. Did he leave, I wonder? Surely, I reason, he would not have left without first waking me.

I lean forward.

'Lee,' I call out, 'where are you? Ulysses, are you here?'

There is no answer, and I listen to the faint sound of the breeze rustling through the leaves; it is my favorite sound. I lean back in the seat and rest a hand on each thigh.

'That damned boy,' I mutter. 'He could have at least told me he was leaving.'

I sit for a while, not moving. I stare into the distance beyond the trees, then to the overgrown yard. So much of my life, it seems, is just this: sitting, staring.

So many dandelions, I think.

Eventually, getting hungry, I move into the house. As I step through the doorway, I stop. From behind me, suddenly, I hear the shrill, quick toot of a whistle. I turn, startled, and look.

At the edge of the yard, near the trees, Ulysses stands, staring at me. He is wearing overalls, stained with dirt, and a white, short-sleeved shirt. In his left hand is a shovel. He is still, silent.

'Ulysses,' I yell, 'what in the Sam Hill are you doing out there?'

He does not move, nor does he speak.

'I thought you left,' I yell. 'I saw your truck was gone and I thought you left.'

Silent, he drops the shovel and begins to walk slowly, as if in a trance, across the yard. As he nears the house, I step forward, curious, watching him, and whisper:

'Good Lord, he looks just like me.'

I raise my head and look out across the rolling field of yellow. Above me, the sky is heavy, rumbling, a rage of black and gray. It will soon rain, I think.

I look down and count the dandelions in my hand; there are eleven. I put one on his chest and one in his hand. I throw two away. I put my fingertips between his cool, dry lips and gently open his mouth.

'I pray for you, all people,' I say. 'And behold my sorrow: my virgins and my young men are gone into captivity. I called for my lovers, but they deceived me: my priests and mine elders gave up the ghost in the city, while they sought their meat to relieve their souls.'

I take four of the dandelions and, one by one, put them in his opened mouth. I close my eyes, then open them, and place a fifth between his parted lips. Holding the remaining two in my hand, I lean back and look at him.

'Goodbye, Dad,' I say.

I raise the two dandelions to my mouth and begin to slowly eat the soft, yellow petals.

I roll over in bed and look at the clock; it is 11:59 a.m. I know where I am, but still I wonder, where am I?

I pull the blanket over my head and close my eyes. My cock is hard; slipping my hands beneath the waistband of my underwear, I hold it with one hand and, with the other, cup my balls.

'Dandelions,' I whisper.

Abruptly, I take my hands from inside my underwear and sit straight. The blanket falls to my lap, and I look down at the small, round scab on my chest. I gently touch it with my thumb; it is sore, tender.

'Oh, Lord,' I say, closing my eyes.

Pushing the blanket aside, I jump out of the bed and hurry

to the window. I stand, looking down into the yard and, across it, into the forest of trees that separate the house, to the left, from the barn and sheds, and, to the right, from the river. I bend forward, opening the window, and lean outside.

'This much I know to be true,' I say, turning back into the room.

I look again at the clock next to the bed; it is a few minutes past noon. I leave the room, then walk quickly downstairs into the kitchen. It is immaculate, bright, sunlight illuminating its every surface and corner.

My suitcase is next to the table, opened, its contents in a jumble; on top is my plane ticket.

'Okay, then,' I say.

I slide a chair from the table and sit down. I close my eyes. The dream returns and, for a moment, I am in a field of dandelions, placing them, one by one, into my father's mouth. Again, I raise my hand to my chest, tracing the wound lightly with my thumb, and say:

'And my father is dead.'

I hunch forward in the chair, folding my arms, and look down at the dull, wooden floor beneath my bare feet. He is dead, I know, and I have buried him. Frightened, suddenly, I sit straight and look out the window.

But how, I wonder, did he die?

The previous evening returns, slowly, in pieces, and I raise my arms to my chest and, as if cold, hug myself. I do not want to be here. I look at the clock on the wall above the refrigerator; it is 12:33 p.m. I close my eyes and begin, slowly, to rock back and forth in the chair.

'Boy,' he says, 'this is your mother.'

I look at the woman; she has the face, I think, of a newly born cat.

'Oh, Permanus,' she says, giggling, 'don't tease the boy like that. Why, he's just the cutest little thing I ever saw.'

She bends forward and touches the back of her hand to my

cheek. She is fat and light-skinned, and her short, nappy hair is the color of straw; she is wearing a pale blue, knee-length dress. She is not my mother, I know, but still, because she is a woman, I like her.

'What's your name, little boy?' she asks.

'Toussaint,' I reply, looking down at the floor.

'Too-saint?'

'Toussaint,' my father says. 'As in L'Ouverture.'

The woman looks at him, then again at me.

'But everyone calls me Toot,' I say.

'Well, that I can pronounce. How old are you, Toot? Nine, ten?'

'No,' I reply, giggling, 'I'm six. But I'll be seven in two weeks.'

'Only six and so big already? Are you telling the truth?'

I nod my head, smiling.

'Well,' she says, 'this much I know to be true: you are just the spitting image of your daddy here.'

I look up at my father and think: No, I'm not.

My father is leaning against the counter; he is drunk. His eyes are red, narrow, and his mouth hangs loose on his face. When my father is drunk, he is nice; he is as nice as he can be.

'Well, Toot,' the woman says, smiling, 'my name is Ruby. And I'm very pleased to meet you.'

She holds out her hand, and I look up at my father.

'Go on,' he says. 'Don't be a baby.'

I put my hand in hers, and, softly, she squeezes it.

'Well, good Lord,' she exclaims. 'That's just about the strongest handshake I've ever felt, Toot. Stronger, even, than your own daddy's, I bet.'

I look up at my father and giggle. He leans forward, ignoring me, and grabs Ruby around the waist. He pulls her backward to his chest; as she pretends to struggle, he cups both of her heavy breasts with his huge hands.

'Oh, Permanus,' she says, giggling, 'not in front of the boy.'

'It's nothing he ain't seen before,' my father replies.

He looks at me as he lowers his head into the crux of her

shoulder and kisses her neck. Behind him, on the wall above the window, is the clock; it is 11:59 p.m.

'Oh, really?' Ruby laughs.

She raises her hand and, rubbing the back of his neck, looks at me and says:

'Maybe you better run along, Toot. Okay, kitten?'

My father's eyes are closed; he kisses her neck and shoulders, running his hands from her breasts down to her hips. As he begins to pull up her skirt, he opens his eyes, suddenly, and looks at me.

'Go on, boy,' he says. 'You should've been in bed a long time ago.'

I stand for a moment, watching them, then turn and walk upstairs to my bedroom. At the top of the stairs, I hear Ruby yell:

'Good night, kitten!'

I do not reply.

I am sitting on the steps of the porch, still in my underwear, staring into the yard. The morning is warm and sunny, windless.

I try to remember, but I am able, it seems, only to forget. I close my eyes, pulling each image, each moment, together, then apart. As in an old movie, I think, the images disappear like pages torn from a calendar; the passage of time no more than fluttering pieces of paper.

I see myself. I see my father. I am talking with him, and then I am burying him. I am wandering through the house, drinking the bourbon; I am in the bathroom, naked, staring at my reflection in the mirror. I see my chest; I see a razor. I see—what do I see?

I see a cigarette.

I am bathing him. I am in the bathtub; I am next to it. I see a hand pulling back my foreskin. I see a wound on his chest—and mine.

I look up, staring out across the yard and down the driveway. I lightly touch my chest and, shaking my head, I whisper:

'It's nothing he ain't seen before.'

I see my grandfather, with my father, at the kitchen table; between them is a book. I see a light-skinned woman with hair the color of straw; next to her is my father and my grandfather. I see a glass of milk, an empty field, a dead dog. Again, I see my father; he is naked.

I look up toward the path that leads into the trees and, further, to his grave. He is in there, I know, wrapped in a sheet and buried in the ground.

I am not a poet, I think. I am a dancer.

Remembering something, then abruptly forgetting it, I stand and walk quickly across the yard and along the path into the trees. Nearing my father's grave, I slow my pace, then suddenly stop. Softly, I say:

'One hundred and seventeen.'

I turn and look back down the narrow, shaded path, not moving, then return quickly toward the grave. Rounding the bend into the small clearing, I stop and look at the mound of dirt.

I remember digging it, but surely it took longer to dig than I remember. It looks so big.

I stand next to the grave. Here he is, I think, a few feet below the surface, naked, wrapped in a sheet, his huge, dark body losing its form and taking another. He is becoming, has become, something different, something rotten, soft: a host.

He is, I realize, no more.

'There are certain things,' he says, 'that a man must never do. And what you won't do is more important than what you will do. Do you understand?'

'Yes, sir,' I lie.

He takes a drink from his coffee cup; it is filled, I know, not with coffee but with whiskey.

'Now,' he continues, wiping his mouth, on either side, with his thumb and forefinger, 'the most important thing is to never lie. But don't get me wrong. I'm not saying to always tell the truth, because there's a difference. Okay?'

I nod my head, watching him.

'Don't just nod your head, boy,' he says. 'I'm trying to teach you something here.'

'Yes, sir,' I reply.

'Okay. Good. Now, the next thing is—well, maybe you're too young to understand this yet, but what you'll learn as you get older, Ulysses, is that you must never, under any circumstance—'

He stops. I watch him, waiting.

'Well,' he says, 'if a woman ever marries you for your money, just make sure she gives you your money's worth. And don't ever hit her.'

He takes a drink from his cup, then says:

'Or love her.'

He laughs.

Why, I wonder, is he laughing?

Belching, he leans back in his chair and rubs his belly.

'And always use your fist when you pick something up. Doesn't matter what it is: a bottle, a pillow, a glass. Hold it like a *man*. Grab it. Do you understand?'

'Yes, sir,' I reply.

'Don't ever go on a diet,' he continues. 'And don't ever buy anything if you can't pay cash for it. On the spot. Oh, and don't ever trust anyone who's worse off than you. You can like them; just don't trust them. You got it?'

'Yes, sir.'

He takes another drink from his cup, then says:

'Good, then go to bed.'

There has been an accident, I am told.

One of two buses carrying ninety-seven freshmen from the state university has crashed; thirty-three of the students are dead. The entire trip has been postponed, and, thus, I am one of only eleven remaining passengers on a flight, first to Frankfurt, then to Casablanca.

'They took a vote,' I hear one of the stewardesses say, 'on

whether to continue with the trip; only half, minus one, wanted to go. Can you believe it?'

'I would've voted to go,' another stewardess says. 'I mean, all that planning and money gone to waste because a few kids couldn't make it. It seems unfair.'

'You are such a bitch,' a third stewardess exclaims. 'God, have some compassion. Besides, now we have less work to do.'

They all laugh.

I look out the window into the darkened sky. Contemptuous, briefly, of the women's remarks, I realize, suddenly, that I see the students' deaths not as a tragedy but as a warning, an omen, of what will happen to *me*. Ashamed, I close my eyes and lean back in the seat.

The stewardesses separate, and I listen to the conversation of a couple three rows ahead, on the opposite side of the airplane. They are arguing.

'Oh, please!' the woman exclaims. 'You only think it's sad because it was in the newspaper. If it was some lounge singer from Savannah, you wouldn't think it was so sad.'

'If it was some lounge singer from Savannah,' the man replies, 'I wouldn't have heard about it. You can't expect me to feel sad about something I don't know.'

'You're missing my point,' the woman says. 'Let's just say that you do read about some lounge singer found dead of an overdose, okay? Let's pretend. You wouldn't feel sad; you'd feel pity. I know you. You'd think he was some pathetic loser, and you'd feel superior to him. Admit it. But because it's Elvis, you think it's, God, almost Shakespearean. That's pathetic. Really, it is.'

'You don't have to exaggerate,' the man replies. 'I didn't say it was Shakespearean. I just said it was sad.'

'You did not just say it was sad. Don't lie. You said it was a tragedy almost symbolic in its depth. Okay? God, you are so pathetic.'

I open my eyes and watch as the woman stands and, grabbing

her purse, walks quickly toward the restroom. She is thin and white, with short, brown hair and masculine features. I imagine my cock in her mouth; her mouth is cool, dry.

My thoughts are interrupted, abruptly, by one of the stewardesses. She smiles, asking if I would like anything to drink.

'A glass of red wine,' I reply.

Still smiling, she asks:

'Merlot or Cabernet Sauvignon?'

'Ripple,' I reply.

'Ripple? I—I don't believe we—'

'I was kidding,' I interrupt. 'Merlot will be fine.'

'Oh,' she says, smiling. 'Okay.'

As she turns, still smiling, and walks away, I am struck by the sudden, strong desire to follow her. Why, I do not know.

I watch her as she returns. Nearing my seat, a tray in her hand, she smiles.

'Here you go,' she says.

I take the glass and small, green bottle of wine, and I thank her.

'If you need anything else,' she says, 'you just let me know.'

'I will,' I say, unscrewing the bottle's cap. 'Thank you.'

Upon arrival in Frankfurt, I am told that the connecting flight to Casablanca has been delayed by seven hours. The clerk, a short, muscular German with sideburns and a nearly flawless command of the English language, offers me a food voucher that is redeemable, he says, at any one of the airport's fine restaurants. I decline the offer, thanking him, and walk to the waiting area.

Along the way, I notice a theater offering pornographic movies. At its entrance, instead of a door, is a red velvet curtain. Passing it, I see a short, thin German soldier walking toward me. He is, I imagine, no older than seventeen. He nods his head at me; I nod in return.

In the waiting area, I sit and read *Bury My Heart at Wounded Knee*. I read three pages and then, unable to concentrate, set the book on the seat beside me. I close my eyes; my grandfather and father stand watching me.

I open my eyes.

I move forward on the seat, resting my elbows on my knees, and clasp my hands. I stare at the pale, gray carpeting and listen to the soft, steady hum of the airport; it comforts me. I have lived much of my adult life, it seems, in airports and train stations and bus depots. They are, I think, my home; I am at home.

'Your grandfather is dead,' he says. 'In his sleep. He died in his sleep.'

'I know,' I reply.

I turn, looking at the man using the telephone next to mine. He is black, with dread locks, wearing a dark blue suit. Flipping through the pages of a datebook that he holds in his hands, he looks at me and smiles; I nod my head, looking away.

'Well,' I hear him say, 'if me can be dere by noon, den me afta cancel. Ras.'

'Ulysses,' my father says. 'Ulysses, are you there?'

'I'm here,' I say, moving the receiver from my right ear to my left ear.

'Well, then, answer me,' my father demands. 'How did you know?'

'Know what?'

'You said you knew that Granddad had died. How? How did you know?'

'I dreamt about it,' I reply, 'the night before last.'

'He died this morning.'

I am anxious, irritated; I want to hang up the phone.

'Well,' I snap, 'I dreamt about it on Friday. I guess I'm clairvoyant, Dad.'

'Don't talk to me like that, boy. Do you hear me?'

I look out across the busy terminal, through the huge windows, at a Boeing jet moving slowly onto the runway.

'I hear you, Dad,' I reply.

He is silent for a moment, and then, softly, he says:

'Well, I wasn't going to tell you 'til you got back, but, seeing as you called, I figured I might as well tell you now.'

'Okay.'

Again, there is silence.

'Dad, listen,' I finally say, 'I better get going. My flight's about to leave and I can't miss it.'

I am lying; my flight does not leave for another hour.

'That's fine,' he replies. 'Just—just call me when you get there. Let me know where I can reach you. Okay?'

I hear the man next to me hang up the phone, and I turn, looking at him.

'What can a brother do?' he says to me, shrugging.

He picks up his briefcase, then turns and rushes into the shifting, steady stream of people. I look down at my wine-colored shoes and think, I need to throw these out.

'Okay, Dad,' I say, 'I'll call you.'

Waiting for him to reply, I realize, slowly, that I am listening to a dial tone; I hang up the phone.

The waiting area is quiet, its few occupants either reading or sleeping. From somewhere around the corner, I hear the drone of a vacuum. I sit in the chair, my arms folded, and look at the waiting area on the opposite side of the terminal; it, too, is silent, still.

I watch a young white man with shoulder-length orange hair and a beard slowly, carefully, pick what I presume to be lint, or hair, from his fuzzy, green turtleneck sweater.

Walking by, I notice the airline clerk who, earlier, had offered me a food voucher; he is carrying a small, red duffel bag. He sees me, smiles, and stops.

'It is a long wait for your plane,' he says.

Is that a question, I wonder, or an observation?

'I've had longer,' I reply, shrugging.

He looks at his watch, then turns his head and looks in the distance. He is silent for a moment, and then, turning toward me, he asks:

'Would you like to talk to me?'

'Would I like to talk to you?' I ask. 'Not particularly. No. Would you like to talk to me?'

'I would,' he replies. 'Yes.'

I shrug, apathetic.

'Would you like for me to sit down?' he asks.

'Hey, man,' I reply, 'you know—whatever.'

He sits in the seat next to mine and smiles. He wants to say something, I can tell, but does not know how to say it. He is nervous.

'You are going to Morocco,' he says. 'Is that correct?'

'It is.'

'Why are you going to Morocco?'

I look at him. He is an ugly man with blunt features and red hair, cut short. A crewcut? His sideburns, thick and neatly groomed, stretch from his ears to the middle of his cheeks.

'I'm performing there,' I answer. 'In Rabat.'

'You are a musician?'

'A dancer.'

'A dancer,' he repeats. 'I see. But if you are performing in Rabat, why are you flying to Casablanca?'

He talks, I think, with the perfect English of a bad actor. I look at the nametag attached to his beige and blue sweater.

'Jurgen,' I say, 'are you a cop?'

'A cop?'

'A police officer.'

'Oh, no,' he laughs, 'I am just curious.'

'Well, don't be.'

'I am sorry,' he says.

He reaches forward and touches me lightly on the shoulder. His hands, I notice, are small and rough, with thick fingers and square, manicured nails; he is wearing a gold wedding band.

'Did I offend you?' he asks.

'No,' I reply, 'you didn't offend me.'

I look at my watch.

'Good,' he says. 'Good.'
He looks behind us, then leans toward me.
'Can I be honest with you?'
'Do what you have to do.'
He is silent, looking at me.
He moves even closer; his breath smells of cigarettes.
'Would you like to make some money?' he asks.
Leaning back, as if to focus properly on his face, I fold my arms and look at him.
'I have enough money,' I reply. 'Thank you.'
Expecting him to respond, I watch him; instead, he bites his lower lip, as if nervous, and continues looking at me. A drug smuggler? I wonder. Or, perhaps, a—what? I do not know.
'Listen,' I say, curious, 'just tell me what's on your mind. Okay?'
He shifts back, slightly, then again moves forward.
'I would like for you to fuck me,' he whispers.
His eyes are pale green, with short, brown lashes. Beneath his left eye is a small, flat mole, colored black.
I say nothing.
'You American black boys,' he says, 'you are beautiful.'
Still, I am silent, looking at his gold wedding band.
'Please,' he says. 'I will pay you.'
I look up at the ceiling.
'Fifty American dollars,' he says.
I look at him; he smiles.
'I know a toilet that is not used; we will be safe there.'
A tall, silver-haired soldier walks by; his stride is slow, straight, and he looks neither to the left nor to the right. In his hands, held against his chest, is a machine gun.
'One hundred dollars,' I say, turning to look at him.
'That is not possible,' he says, frowning.
I shrug.
'How about—' he begins to say.
'One hundred dollars,' I interrupt, not looking at him.

'Are you sure?' he asks.

I look at him but say nothing,

He looks down, as if thinking, then nods his head.

'All right,' he says, looking up. 'All right. One hundred dollars. I will give you one hundred dollars.'

I stand, grabbing my bag, and pass it to him.

'Carry it,' I say.

He takes the bag, and I follow him as he leads me through the terminal.

At the end of a long, narrow corridor, down an escalator, around a corner, and through a pair of swinging doors, is a hallway; at the end of the hallway is a door and, to its left, is another. On the door, at eye level, is a sign that reads *'Nur für Angestellte.'*

We enter the restroom and lock the door behind us. I watch in silence as the man sets down his bag, and mine, and looks at me.

He is bowlegged, short, and muscular; I am reminded of a bulldog. Behind him is a sink and mirror; in its reflection, over his shoulder, I see my face.

'I want to suck you first,' he says.

I look at him.

'Go ahead,' I say, not moving.

He walks toward me, kneels, and, wrapping his arms around my waist, begins to rub the side of his face against my crotch and stomach.

'*Schöner Junge,*' he murmurs.

I stand, looking at my reflection in the mirror.

'Beautiful black boy,' I hear him whisper, 'let me love you.'

I look down at him and say:

'Why?'

In my father's closet, hidden beneath a stack of neatly folded overalls, is a hardback book of poetry. On its red cover, in large, white letters, are the words, *'Seed* by Toussaint Dove.'

Of the seventy-three pages, there are four that are missing: the thirty-first, the thirty-second, the thirty-fifth, and the thirty-sixth. On the thirty-third page is a poem: 'Hymn.' Its last four lines are:

> And I beg of you, please,
> You strange and vengeful God,
> Judge me not for what I can never do
> And forgive me for what I can.

Grasping the side of the sink with both hands, he rests his forehead against the mirror and says:
'*Bitte. Bitte.*'
I look at his face; his eyes are closed.
'*Bitte,*' he whispers. '*Größer, Neger*—nigger. *Bitte.*'
I look down at his pale, freckled back.
'*Schöner Junge,*' he says, opening his eyes. '*Lieben Sie mich?*'
Ignoring him, I spread his buttocks and place the head of my cock against his puckered, red asshole.
'Please,' he murmurs, closing his eyes and gently raising his hips.
I shove it in.
He opens his eyes.
I pull out my cock and, again, shove it in.
Arching his back, he rises and tries to pull away from me.
'Halt!' he yells.
I grab his hips, roughly pulling him back, and continue to fuck him with short, hard strokes. I stop, pulling my cock out, then shove it in again. Still, he struggles, and with my left hand, I reach up and grab him around the neck, pushing his face against the mirror.
'Silence,' I hear someone say. 'We must have silence.'
Startled, I look in the mirror, then behind me; no one is there.
I turn my head back and look again, over the man's shoulder, at my reflection.
'*Bitte,*' he pleads. 'Halt. Halt. Stop.'
'Take a deep breath,' I say, staring at my reflection. 'It won't hurt as much.'

I glance at the man's face; his eyes are closed and he is crying. Over and over, he repeats:

'*Bitte.*'

Soon, he becomes limp, silent.

'Good boy,' I whisper, as if to myself.

Letting go of his neck, I grab him by the hair, pulling him up and back, and smash his face into the mirror; the mirror cracks. He turns, a drop of blood running slowly down the center of his pale face, and looks at me. He asks:

'Why?'

I realize, suddenly, that I have forgotten my book in the waiting area. I let go of him, stepping back, and ejaculate onto the floor.

'Why not?' I reply.

I look at the date of publication and, setting the book in my lap, begin to add, then subtract. Again, I look at the date.

'Nineteen,' I whisper.

He was nineteen.

I put the book beneath the stack of overalls, then stand and quickly leave my father's bedroom.

'Nineteen.'

I go downstairs and walk into the kitchen. The curtain above the sink has been drawn and the room is dark, cool. Through the screen door I can see the dog, in the yard, chasing a butterfly.

I step out onto the verandah and walk slowly toward the barn. It is a bright, hot day and I am lazy. But he will soon be home, I think, and if my chores are not done, I will, in his words, be ass over tea kettle. I hurry into the barn and begin raking the stalls.

Midway through the first of the four stalls, I stop, resting my elbow on the rake, and look up at the rough, wooden ceiling.

'Nineteen,' I say.

I lift the rake and, holding it high, brush the cobwebs from between two of the huge beams. I lower the rake and resume my work. I have never even seen him read, I think. Much less write.

'All those letters strung together,' he has said. 'For what?'

Again stopping, I hold the rake, staring at its smooth, wooden handle. How, then, I wonder, is it possible that he once wrote, and published, an entire book of poetry? It confuses me.

'Still pissing around, I see,' I hear him say.

I turn, startled, and see that he is standing in the doorway of the barn. He is wearing overalls; over his left shoulder, he balances a gunnysack of oats.

'I didn't hear you drive up,' I say. 'You scared me.'

'I'm sure I did,' he replies.

He leans forward, letting the sack of oats slip off his shoulder into his outstretched arms. He turns, carrying the sack like a baby, and begins walking toward the house.

'Just get busy,' I hear him say. 'You have a lot to do today.'

The festival has been cancelled. Though I will not be paid, I am told, I will be reimbursed for my travelling expenses. Albeit customary, even regulatory, that an artist be paid for a cancelled performance, I do not protest. If anything, I am relieved that I will not be dancing.

Not wanting to remain in Rabat, I take the train to Tangier; I have been there before. It is a long ride, passing again through Casablanca, and I sleep most of the way. Upon arrival, I take a taxi to the Medina. At its entrance, I get out and walk the remaining distance to my hotel.

The Medina's streets are narrow, paved with brick, and bordered on either side by tall, crumbling buildings colored white, red, yellow, rust, gray. Built on a slope, the ancient, enclosed neighborhood rises and falls, its busy streets abruptly turning, ending, beginning.

I am approached along the way by countless men, young and old, attempting, sometimes physically, to sell me any number of goods and services; I refuse them all.

At the hotel, I ask for a room overlooking the courtyard. It is a small hotel, once grand, with marble floors and high, dark, wooden walls. Abderahim, the clerk, tells me that a room overlooking the courtyard is not available. Instead, he offers me another, also on the second floor, that is, he says, just as comfortable. I do not believe him, but still I accept.

'Have you been here before, sir?' he asks, passing me the key to my room.

I look at his dark, bearded face.

'Well,' he demands, 'have you?'

I look down at the key in my hand, then gaze out the opened door onto the narrow street. Suddenly, I am tired.

'Yes,' I reply, looking up at his face, 'I have.'

The room is small, with a gray, stone floor and pink walls. There is a sink, a desk, a closet, and a metal-framed bed. Next to the sink is a window. It reminds me, I think, of a hospital: cold and clean, without adornment.

I close the door and set my bag on the bed. I look out the window; below me is a narrow street, almost a path, really, that to my left runs into the Petit Socco, a small, brown-bricked square bordered by cigarette shops, open-air cafés, and crumbling hotels. I am reminded, briefly, of the dark, narrow hallways of my father's house.

It is early afternoon and the square is quiet. I watch a young boy, wearing a brown djellaba and red jelly slippers, push a small, wooden wheelbarrow of fresh mint through the center of the square, then disappear into one of the narrow, shadowed side streets.

I turn from the window, closing it, and walk to the bed. I put my bag on the floor and undress. I lie down, tired, and fall asleep until midnight.

'Maybe you're just rotten,' he says. 'Have you ever thought of that?'

I look at him; he looks at me.

'Have you?' he asks. 'Have you ever, even once, thought of that?'

I remain silent, watching him. He rests his huge, dark hands on the table between us. But for the index finger of his left hand, which ends in a stump at the knuckle, his hands remind me, have reminded me since boyhood, of a horse's foot and hoof: hump-knuckled, scarred, with thick, square fingernails that are cracked and blackened.

'Because maybe, just maybe,' he continues, 'that's the answer. It's not me. It's not what I did or didn't do. It's not your—not that you never knew your mother. It's not your grandfather. It's just you. Have you thought of that? Have you? That it was you, Ulysses, dead and rotting, rotten, right from the womb?'

Still, I say nothing. When he is dead and buried, I think, it will be his hands that I remember.

'Well,' he demands, 'have you?'

I look out the window above the sink, then turn my head, slowly, and again look at his hands. Both thumbs, as if broken, curve outward from the knuckle at nearly ninety-degree angles.

'Have you?'

'Yes,' I reply, looking up at his face, 'I have.'

I lie in bed, upon waking, and stare at the ceiling. Outside my door, down the hall, I can hear two Americans, a man and a woman, arguing.

'I don't care,' the man says. 'There was something creepy about it.'

'Creepy? Oh, please. He was just trying to make some money, for God's sake,' the woman replies.

In each of their voices, I notice a slight New England accent.

'I know he was,' the man says. 'But I didn't feel right about it.'

'You are so provincial, Jonathan. Really, you are.'

'Maybe so. But better that than some—some ugly American getting his shoes shined in the middle of the night by a seven-year-old kid.'

'A seven-year-old kid who needed the money; don't forget that. Okay? Your little guilt trip probably cost that kid a meal.'

'Oh, please.'

'It's true. What's five dirham to you? Fifty cents? To him it's—it's a bottle of olive oil and a loaf of bread. If not more.'

'Well, he got it, didn't he? What'd you give him? Ten dirham?'

'That's not the point.'

'Well, what is the point, Maggie? Huh? Just tell me; I'm tired. I want to go to bed.'

'The point, Jonathan, is that you can't bring your American sensibilities to another country and expect everyone to follow suit. They have their way of doing things and we have ours.'

Silence.

'Refusing to respect the way they do things,' she continues, 'is no different than—than what the colonizers did. God. It's still a case of trying to shove your ideology down someone else's throat. Can't you see that?'

'No,' the man replies. 'I can't.'

'Well, it is. Trust me. That kid couldn't give a shit about your fucking morality. He just wanted to make some money so he could eat.'

'Or buy some weed. I mean, what's a seven-year-old kid doing up at midnight, anyway?'

'Oh, okay,' the woman groans. 'So, that's what this is all about. I should've known. There you are trying to pretend it's a matter of ethics when, really, it's just because you were disgusted by him.'

'I didn't say that.'

'No, but that's what you meant. You thought he was a little hoodlum.'

'Don't tell me what I meant, Maggie. Okay? Just don't tell me what I do or don't mean. It pisses me off.'

'I'm sure it does. *What's a seven-year-old kid doing up at midnight, anyway?* God. What do you think he was doing, you asshole? Buying crack?'

'You don't have to be so dramatic, Maggie. I didn't say he was going to—'

'I'm not being dramatic,' she interrupts. 'I'm being sarcastic. Okay? There's a difference.'

'Whatever.'

'Whatever?'

'Yes,' the man replies, sighing. 'Whatever.'

'You know,' the woman replies, 'why don't you just go fuck yourself?'

I am reminded, briefly, of the couple on the plane, arguing about Elvis, and I am thankful, suddenly, to be single.

'You don't have to swear,' I hear the man say.

'No, but I want to,' the woman replies. 'Is that all right with you, *asshole?*'

I hear a door slam, and then silence.

I lie in bed for a moment, then sit up. I get dressed, not bothering to turn on the light, and put on my shoes. I open the window, leaning outside; it is warm and the sky is clear and dark.

A gray cat walks slowly down the middle of the street below me and into the silent, empty square. It stops, sits, and looks around. I watch it for a moment, then turn and shut the window.

Leaving my room, I lock the door, then put the key in my pocket. As I walk down the hallway, I see a young black woman in the distance, leaning over the rail and looking into the courtyard.

I walk through the narrow, poorly lit hall and step down onto the balcony that surrounds the courtyard; on its opposite side is the stairway to the front desk.

As I near the woman, she turns and smiles at me. What a beautiful woman, I think. She is young, perhaps twenty-five, tall and slender, long-limbed, with dark skin and long hair, pulled back and tied in a twist. She wears a floor-length orange skirt, leather sandals, and, over her shoulders, a translucent purple scarf.

As I pass her, I nod my head and smile; she looks away.

'That must be jelly,' I hear her say, ''cause jam sure don't shake like that.'

'Excuse me,' I reply, stopping.

She continues to rest, arms folded, against the railing; turning her head, she looks at me.

'You didn't just say that,' I ask, 'did you?'

She winks at me and says:

'Just playing with you, big boy; don't worry.'

I study her face, curious.

'I'm not worried,' I reply.

'Then what are you?' she asks.

Is she drunk? I wonder.

'Just curious,' I reply.

'Aren't we all,' she says.

She lowers her head, turning, and looks down into the courtyard.

'That sounded corny,' she remarks. 'Didn't it? *Aren't we all?* I hate when people say that; like they're some—some kind of world-weary genius. It's so pretentious.'

I shrug, looking at the back of her long, slender neck.

She turns her head, gazing up at me, as if suddenly suspicious, and asks:

'So, where are you going?'

I continue to look at her, and ask:

'Why?'

'Calm down; I'm just asking. The front door is locked, you know?'

'Already?'

I look down into the courtyard and think: It's not even a courtyard, just a marble fountain, really, surrounded by a short, wrought-iron gate.

'The guy who works at the front desk,' the woman asks, 'what's his name?'

'Abderahim,' I reply. 'Why?'

'He'll open the front door for you.'

I smile.

'I know,' I say. 'I've been here before.'

'So you also know that he gets pissed off about it?'

I nod my head.

'But he gets pissed off about everything,' I say.

She steps away from the balcony and, folding her arms, turns toward me.

'What's your name?' she asks.

'Ulysses,' I reply.

'Well, Ulysses, I'm Maggie.'

'As in Margaret?'

'As in Magdelena.'

'Hey, was that you out here a few minutes ago,' I ask, 'arguing with your boyfriend?'

'You heard that?' she responds. 'Sorry.'

'Don't worry about it. It was interesting. Kind of.'

'To you, maybe. To me, it was boring. And he's not my boyfriend.'

'Actually,' I say, 'you sounded more like a married couple.'

'What an awful thing to say,' she replies, frowning.

Slowly, she smiles.

'Unfortunately, though,' she says, 'you're probably right.'

'You know,' I reply, 'when I was listening to you two talk, I was sure I could hear a New England accent. But now I don't.'

'Well, he's from Boston, so I'm sure you did. But not me; I'm a Brooklyn girl.'

'Brooklyn? I don't hear that either.'

She laughs softly and says:

'Thank God.'

Suddenly, she frowns again.

'What's wrong?' I ask.

'I told myself not to say that anymore.'

'Say what?'

'*Thank God.* I hate when people say that. I mean, who thanks God for anything anymore? It's such an exaggeration. Well, except with Muslims, maybe. And Rastafarians.'

'Okay,' I reply, watching her. '*Aren't we all?* and *Thank God.* What else aren't you supposed to say?'

She looks at me and bites her lip.
'You must think I'm crazy.'
'Not yet.'
'Well,' she says, 'stick around.'
'Maybe I will.'
She is silent for a moment, watching me, then asks:
'Are you flirting with me?'
'No. Would you like me to?'
'Not particularly,' she says.
'Good,' I reply. 'So now we know.'
She smiles, folding her slender arms across her chest.
'So,' she says, 'you still haven't told me where you were going. *Are* going.'
'I don't know,' I answer. 'Just for a walk.'
She puts her hands on her hips,
'You want some company, sailor?'
'Well, I don't know. You seem a little—'
'Don't say it,' she warns.
There is silence as we stand staring at one another; we smile.
'Well, what about your friend?' I ask.
'Jonathan,' she says. 'Oh, please. He's probably in bed jacking off to *Coming of Age in Samoa*.'
I look at her.
'Oh my God, I'm awful,' she says. 'Isn't that awful?'
She looks at me, mock terror on her face, then winks and takes my arm.
'C'mon,' she says. 'Let's go.'

He walks into my room and throws a large brown envelope on the bed.
'What is this?' he asks.
I look up at his face, then at the envelope. I stretch across the bed and pick up the envelope. It is addressed to him, opened; inside is a passport and a white piece of paper, folded in half.

'Oh,' I say, looking at him, 'I applied for a passport. Remember? You said it was—'

'Look at it,' he says.

'I did,' I reply.

'Take it out,' he demands. 'And open it and *look* at it.'

I do as he says, resting the envelope in my lap. Opening the passport, I look at the picture, then at the name, then at my father.

'How did that happen?' I ask.

'You tell me,' he replies.

Again, I look at the passport; though there is a black-and-white photograph of myself, my father's name, birthdate, and particulars are contained within.

I look up at him.

'I have no idea,' I say. 'I filled out all the information and—'

'And put down my name, instead of yours,' he interrupts. 'Along with height and weight and date of birth.'

'I didn't, Dad. I swear.'

'Then how did it get in there? I never filled out the application; you did.'

'I—I don't know. I must have—I don't know.'

He looks at me, frowning, then shakes his head.

'Well,' he says, 'it's not like you were going anywhere, anyway.'

He steps forward, grabbing the passport from my hand, and rips it in half. Throwing the pieces in my lap, he turns toward the door, then stops.

'I don't know how you did it,' he says, looking at me, 'but if you ever pull a stunt like that again, you'll be sorry. Do you understand me?'

I nod my head.

'You may be seventeen,' he continues, 'but I can still get you where it hurts, boy. Trust me.'

I watch as he turns, leaving the room.

'But I didn't do it,' I whisper, looking at the torn passport in my lap.

'As much as I love this city,' she says, 'it also frightens me.'

We are walking through the quiet, shadowed streets of the Medina. We are walking simply to walk, with neither direction nor destination in mind.

'The people,' I ask, 'they frighten you?'

'Oh, no, not at all,' she replies. 'The city itself. I always feel as if it's closing in on me. You know? It's the same in New York, but there it's because of all the people. And how huge everything is. But here, it's—it's like being in an old house. You know?'

'A very old house,' I say, 'with very narrow hallways.'

'And no windows,' she adds.

It is what it is, I think: an old, two-story farmhouse in which the owner has recently died.

She is silent, for a moment, then asks:

'So, why do I love it here, I wonder?'

I turn my head as we walk and look at her.

'I don't know,' I say. 'Why do you love it here?'

She folds her arms, as if to caress herself.

'Because I'm crazy,' she replies, smiling. 'I mean, no one ever stays here anymore; they just pass through on their way to Marrakech or Fes or—or Essaouira.'

'Maybe that's why you love it,' I say, 'because no one else does.'

'Maybe,' she says, sighing. 'But I'd hate to think that's why. I mean, it is a beautiful city, too. Right? Well, some of it, anyway.'

We walk up a flight of crumbling stone steps, then turn, walking down a short, narrow street and around a corner. Up another flight of steps, we enter a small square, at its center a brick well and water pump, and, again, down a short, narrow street that ends, abruptly, at the Medina's huge wall.

We then turn and continue the way we came.

'You're not tired,' she asks, 'are you?'

'Not at all,' I reply. 'Why?'

'Do you want to leave the Medina? Maybe get a drink somewhere?'

'Sure,' I say. 'The El Minzah has a bar; have you been there?'

'Fuck the El Minzah,' she says. 'All those bloody Spanish businessmen and old fairies. Let's go somewhere else.'

'Well,' I say, 'lead on.'

As we walk, she takes a small, red-sequined purse from beneath her scarf and retrieves a joint and a brass lighter; once lit, she takes a few puffs, then hands the joint to me.

'Want some?' she asks.

Her fingers, I notice, are long and slender, with perfect, oval-shaped fingernails, painted dark red.

'What is it?' I ask.

'Crack,' she replies. 'What the hell does it look like?'

'Hey, I don't smoke anything unless—'

'I'm just playing with you,' she interrupts. 'It's weed, just plain old weed.'

I take the joint and, when finished, hand it back to her.

'You smoke like a girl,' she says, taking a puff.

'And you smoke like a boy,' I reply.

She smiles, trying not to cough, and again passes me the joint.

Two men wearing djellabas, hoods pulled over their heads, pass by; they are silent, moving quickly, the hems of their long, dark robes brushing the ground as they walk. How odd, I think, that the djellabas are so long; traditionally, they are ankle-length.

'Whenever I see someone in one of those robes with the hood pulled up,' she says, 'I always imagine them to have cat's eyes. Especially at night, when you can't see their faces.'

I smile, handing her the joint; it is nearly finished.

'Jonathan bought one,' she says. 'I told him he looks like an idiot wearing it, but he refuses to listen to me. You look like a druid, I told him. Or like Yoda, from *Return of the Jedi*.'

I am tempted, briefly, to ask of her relationship with Jonathan, but I do not. If she wants to tell me, I reason, she will.

'Here,' she says. 'There's a little left.'

She passes me the joint; taking a few, quick puffs, I drop the roach on the ground. We continue walking.

Stepping through the Medina's entrance into the Grand Socco, I glance at Maggie; arms folded beneath her chest, she walks slowly, elegantly, her head held high. Like a queen, I think, surveying her domain.

She has, I now notice, draped the large, purple scarf over her hair and across her shoulders. She looks at me and smiles, then stares ahead into the wide, open space of the Grand Socco.

We move slowly, silently, along the periphery of the darkened square; in its center, on one of several benches, sits a young, bearded man who watches us as we walk. He is smoking a cigarette. Far behind him, on the Grand Socco's opposite side, I see two small cars, side by side, with flashing headlights.

Is it a signal, I wonder?

Suddenly, I hear Maggie laughing; I look at her.

'Why are you blinking like that?' she asks, her arms still folded.

'Was I blinking?' I ask.

'Yes, you were blinking.'

'Am I still doing it?' I ask, looking at her.

'No,' she says, laughing softly, 'you're not still doing it.'

'Damn,' I say. 'Are you sure that was just weed we smoked?'

She smiles slyly and says:

'As far as I know.'

'Well, I hope so,' I say.

She moves closer to me, slipping her arm through mine, and says:

'Just relax.'

I stand on the verandah, looking through the screen door at my father and grandfather; they are seated across from each other at the kitchen table. Either they do not see me or they are simply ignoring me.

My grandfather is leaning forward, one arm stretched across the table as if reaching for something, the other at his side. My father sits, his arms folded, and stares at the table.

'It belongs to me,' my grandfather says. 'It's mine.'

He is angry.

'I know that,' my father replies. 'Just relax. It's not—'

'Don't you tell me to relax,' my grandfather demands. 'I am relaxed.'

They look at one another, silent.

'I'm here,' my father says, calmly. 'And Ulysses is here, and we—hell, Dad, Ulysses is only eleven and he does just as much around here as you do. Even more.'

'As well he should,' my grandfather says. 'No reason that little nigger shouldn't.'

I put my hands in my pockets.

'I'm not saying he shouldn't,' my father replies. 'I'm just saying that if this farm is going to be mine, anyway, and—and if me and my boy are—'

'I ain't in my grave yet, mister,' my grandfather interrupts, inching forward in his seat. 'And until I am, this farm is mine, with my rules.'

My father slowly shakes his head.

'You go on,' my grandfather says. 'Make any face you want. But you're still going to have to wait 'til I'm dead and buried before you start making up any rules around here. You understand?'

My father looks at him, saying nothing.

'Then it'll be your boy's turn,' my grandfather continues, 'to complain about what you will or won't let him do. That's just how it goes, Toussaint. If you don't like it, leave.'

'And then what would you do?' my father asks, laughing softly. 'You can barely walk down those stairs in the morning, let alone do the chores by yourself.'

'Maybe so, but I can just as well hire someone who will. You're not the only dumb ox around; don't think you are.'

'Oh, Lord!' my father exclaims. 'Who in the hell could you find to come all the way out here to work like a horse for pennies a day?'

'Don't you worry about that. There's a lot of men out there who'd be thankful to work an honest day's work and—and have a roof over their head and a belly full of food.'

'This isn't the slave days, old man. No one wants to work sixteen hours a day for food and shelter and then be told what they can and can't do, especially if one of the things they can't do is get a woman every now and again.'

'You want to get laid,' my grandfather scoffs, sitting back in his chair, 'you go right ahead. But you ain't bringing any whore around here. You find someplace else.'

I listen to the two of them argue, looking down at my bare, dusty feet.

'I wasn't bringing a whore,' my father replies, sternly. 'I was bringing a lady I—'

'A lady? Then what do you need to bring her out here for?'

'What do you think? Dinner—conversing.'

'You can have dinner in town. And you can converse and—and get laid there, too.'

'Hell, Dad, it's not like I was planning on having sex with her here on the kitchen table. I invited her for dinner. That's all.'

'I don't care,' my grandfather replies. 'Look what happened with the last woman you brought out here. You knocked her up, married her, and soon as Ulysses was born she went and run off on the two of you.'

I look up.

'And so what if she did?' my father says. 'That's my business, not yours.'

'It's my farm,' my grandfather says. 'It's my business.'

They become silent, staring at one another. I am about to turn and leave when my father finally speaks. He says:

'Your business? Like when I was a boy and you'd bring a different woman home every weekend?'

My grandfather tilts back his head, slightly, and smiles.

'You're full of shit, Toussaint,' he says. 'Right full up to your chink eyes with shit.'

What, I wonder, is a chink?

'Don't tell me you forgot about all those women,' my father says. 'You don't remember them, Dad? Huh? One yellow gal after the other; you'd take them upstairs and I'd—'

My grandfather stands, knocking the chair backwards onto the floor.

'That's a lie,' he says. He is no longer smiling.

'What about Ruby?' my father says, ignoring him. 'Do you remember her, perhaps? Fat and yellow, with straw-blond hair? Do you remember her, Dad? Do you remember when she snuck into my room while you were sleeping and—'

Startling me, my grandfather leans over the table and smacks my father across the mouth. I step backward, nearly stumbling, but quickly gain my balance and take a single step forward, watching.

My father sits for a moment, as if stunned, then raises his left hand and wipes the trickle of blood from his bottom lip; he begins to speak but, for some reason, does not.

'You're a damned liar,' my grandfather says, calmly. 'You always were.'

He turns and begins walking toward the screen door. I quickly step away and run down the steps and out into the yard. Behind me, I hear the screen door open, then close. I do not look back.

It is early afternoon; I am sitting at one of the sidewalk cafés in the Petit Socco, drinking a cup of peppermint tea.

It is raining softly, and though the square is nearly empty of pedestrians, the café is bustling and noisy, crowded. The air is thick with smoke; above the din is the sound of a football game on the television in the corner. It rests high on the wall, atop a shelf near the ceiling.

I sit quietly, listening to the mostly incomprehensible conversations of the men around me and looking at the dark, dusty, yellow walls and water-stained ceiling.

In the corner, below the black-and-white television set, a bearded man wearing a black djellaba sits alone, smoking a wooden pipe and staring angrily at me.

I nod my head; he looks away. I take a drink of the hot, sweet tea. What I should do, I think, is stand, walk to his table, pull out my cock, and piss on him.

'Or fuck him,' I whisper, setting the cup on the table.

'Hey, you freak,' I hear a woman say.

I look up; it is Maggie. She is alone, wearing an outfit similar to the previous night's: long skirt, sandals, a scarf over her hair and around her shoulders. She smiles, sitting down.

'Did you just wake up?' she asks, looking through the crowd of men and waving at the middle-aged man behind the counter.

The man nods his head and waves, as if to dismiss her.

'Asshole,' she says, looking at me. 'I come in here every day and that bastard acts like the only time he's ever seen me is down by the docks giving head to the sailors. God. I wear this fucking scarf out of respect; you'd think I could get a little in return!'

'You want me to go get you something?' I ask, looking at the man.

'Oh, no, that's okay. He'll be over here any minute now,' she says, rolling her eyes. 'He just wants me to know what a dirty, diseased whore I am. It's the same thing every day.'

'Then why do you come back?' I ask.

'Because I like it here,' she replies, shrugging.

I look at her.

I wasn't bringing a whore, I think. I was bringing a lady.

'So, you didn't answer my question,' she says. 'Did you just wake up? Your eyes are all puffy.'

'Are they?'

'They are.'

'Well, yes, I did just get up.'

'I should hope so. You were as high as, well, I don't want to say a kite but—you were high, my brother.'

I should hope so. Why, I wonder?

She leans forward, resting her elbows on the small, wobbly table between us, and smiles.

'Or do you even remember last night?' she asks.

Beneath the table, she pushes her knee against mine.

'Of course I remember last night,' I reply.

She kicks me lightly in the shin, then leans back in the chair and folds her slender arms across her chest. She says:

'So do I.'

Just then, the man from behind the counter walks up to us and abruptly sets a cup and metal pot of tea on the table. Before we can say anything, he turns and makes his way back through the crowded, smoky café.

'Cocksucker,' Maggie whispers, leaning forward and opening the small pot's lid. 'Just like I thought, half full.'

She shrugs, pouring the tea, then again folds her arms and rests her elbows on the table. She is no longer wearing nail polish, I notice.

'So,' she says, smiling mischievously, 'is there anything you want to take back?'

'Take back?'

Over her shoulder, I can see that the man beneath the television is, again, staring at me. He is, however, no longer alone; across from him, looking up at the television, is a man wearing a rust-colored djellaba and a New York Yankees baseball cap, worn backwards.

'Well?' Maggie says.

I look at her.

'Sometimes,' she says, 'we say and do things when we're high that we later regret.'

Puzzled, I look at her and ask:

'What are you talking about?'

'I thought you said you remember last night,' she replies, taking a sip of the tea.

'I do remember last night, and I don't remember doing or

saying anything I want to take back. Is there something *you* want to take back?'

'Not at all.'

'Good. Me neither.'

I raise my cup of tea, as if to toast her, then take a drink.

She sits, watching me, then tilts her head to the left and smiles.

'Do you remember,' she asks, 'telling me that you murdered your father?'

I set down the cup.

'Did I say that?' I ask.

'So, you don't remember last night, then?'

'Not that, I don't. Well—'

My mind begins to spin, pulling together the minutes, moments, of our previous night's conversation.

'You sure did,' she says. 'Among other things.'

I look at her.

'Like what?' I ask.

She laughs softly, then says:

'God, I can't even remember it all. Brotherman, you sure like to talk when you're high.'

She lets out a long, soft whistle; the three men at the table on our left turn and look at her, then at me, and then away.

'No, I don't,' I say. 'I don't like to talk, period.'

'Well, last night you did. That's for certain.'

My mind still spinning, working to remember, I look at her.

'Well,' I say, 'can you give me an example?'

'Tell you what,' she says, reaching beneath her scarf and retrieving her small, red-sequined purse, 'let's play a game.'

She takes a pack of Gitanes from the purse, lights one, and rests back in her chair. Inhaling, then slowly exhaling, she looks at me.

'And what game is that?' I ask, slightly irritated.

'True or false,' she replies. 'I'll tell you what you said, and now that your mind is—is clear—you can tell me if it's true or false.'

I smile and say:

'Okay. Shoot.'

She looks up at the ceiling, then down. She takes another drag of her cigarette. On the middle finger of her right hand is a huge turquoise and silver ring.

'Your name is Ulysses Dove,' she says. 'You don't have a middle name.'

'True.'

'Your father's name was Toussaint. And your grandfather's name was Permanus.'

'True,' I reply.

'They were both coalminers and, for a while, so were you.'

'False.'

She giggles.

'Okay, then. You're a dancer.'

'That's true.'

'You came to Morocco to dance at a festival in Rabat, but it was cancelled and you came here. To—to rest.'

'True. Basically.'

'When you were a boy,' she says, 'you used to like to eat dirt.'

'True. And I still do.'

'You don't eat red meat, normally, but sometimes you eat goat. Curry goat.'

I smile.

'True,' I say.

She smiles as well, taking a drag of her cigarette. Without moving her head, she looks at the men next to us, then again at me.

'You spent four years in prison for armed robbery.'

I look at her.

'Did I say that?' I ask.

'Just answer the question.'

'Well, false.'

She smiles.

'I was just testing you,' she says. 'You never said that.'

I lean forward, frowning, and pretend to knock her on the side of the head.

'Okay,' she says. 'Next one.'
'Go for it.'
'You were raised by your father and grandfather.'
'True. Unfortunately.'
'Your father wrote a book of poetry that he never told you about.'
'True.'
'Okay. You never knew your mother.'
'True.'
'Your father never knew his.'
'True.'

She raises her cigarette and, inhaling, looks at me. She is silent for a while, continuing to look at me, and then, softly, she says:

'Sometimes you black out, and when you come to, you don't remember what you did.'

'True. Kind of. I mean, sometimes I just get so wrapped up in my thoughts that I forget where I am. But, no, I don't actually black out.'

'Well,' she says, 'that's not what you said last night. You said you blacked out. So, that's your first lie.'

I smile at her.

'Let's just call it a misunderstanding,' I say.

She frowns, then says:

'Next question.'
'Okay. Go for it.'
'Your favorite singer is Nina Simone.'
I smile.
'True,' I say.

'That's funny,' she says, giggling. 'I was sure that one was false. Brothers always lie about their favorite singers. Saying they like Nina and—and Phyllis Hyman—just to impress a sister.'

'Well,' I say, 'it's true.'
'Okay. If you say so.'
'Next.'
'Next,' she repeats, pausing for a moment.
I watch her.

'Well,' she says, 'you killed your father—you didn't say how—and you buried him in the woods by your house.'
'False.'
She looks at me, her eyes narrowed, and asks:
'Are you sure?'
I smile.
'I hope so,' I say. 'He's dead and—and I buried him. Let's just leave it at that.'
We sit, looking at one another. I glance at the man below the television; he is sleeping. I look again at Maggie as she takes a drag of her cigarette and stares at me suspiciously.
'I think you did it,' she says.
'Did what?' I ask.
'Killed your father.'
I shrug, thinking, Who cares?
'Are you going to turn me in?' I ask.
She smiles.
'No,' she says. 'I've never known anyone who's killed their father before.'
'Well, now you do. Congratulations.'
Still she smiles.
'Has anyone ever told you that you're a very unemotional man?' she asks.
'As a matter of fact,' I reply, 'yes.'
'That's typical of murderers, you know.'
'I doubt that,' I say. 'Maybe serial killers, but I'm sure most murderers are—well, why would we kill someone unless it was based on—unless it was a result of emotion?'
'For fun,' she replies, smiling.
'Not a father,' I reply. 'No one murders their father for fun. Out of necessity, perhaps, but not for fun.'
'You're quite the expert, my brother,' she says, 'for someone who didn't do it.'
'Who said I didn't do it?' I ask.
'You.'

'But I thought I said I did do it,' I reply, 'last night.'

'So cold,' she says, shaking her head. 'So cold. You laugh. Softly, of course. And I bet you sometimes show your anger. But that's it. Right?'

She drops her cigarette on the floor and crushes it with the heel of her sandal. Around her ankle, I notice, is a thin, silver chain.

'What else is there,' I ask, 'besides anger and laughter?'

'Sadness,' she replies. 'Vulnerability. Pity. Joy. Jealousy. Frustration. Fear. A lot of things.'

'A man can feel something,' I say, 'without expressing it. Just because he doesn't show it doesn't mean he doesn't feel it. And just because someone *does* show it doesn't necessarily mean he, or she, feels it.'

She raises her eyebrows.

'Maybe,' she says.

'And just because I don't express it,' I say, 'doesn't mean I'm ashamed of it, either. Maybe I just want to keep it to myself.'

'Like admitting that you killed your father? You want to keep that to yourself?'

'If I really killed him, do you think I'd tell a woman I just met?'

'Hey, you don't even remember telling me.'

'Maybe I do and I'm just saying I don't.'

Again, she smiles.

'And even if I did do it,' I say, 'what does it matter? We're in Tangier. Nothing matters in Tangier.'

She looks at the men next to us, and again at me.

'Nothing matters,' she says. 'To an *American* in Tangier. That's why we're here, right?'

We sit, looking at each other, and smile.

'That's right,' I reply.

I look up at my father; he is looking away, above my head, into the clear, summer sky. The preacher, a light-skinned black man with freckles and red hair, looks at the large pine coffin at the grave's bottom and says:

'Dirt. This is what we are. We come from dirt; we return to it. And here, now, on this glorious summer Sabbath we say goodbye to yet another, Lord.

'His body, like all bodies, is where it belongs now. Yes, Lord. This is where it all, it *all,* belongs, deep in the earth, the dirt, the soil, from which all earthly life arises.'

But what about fish? I wonder.

'This is where we belong, Lord,' he continues. 'But his soul, his spirit, Lord, his soul—it is free. And it is this freedom that frightens us—not the physical death so much as the spiritual freedom. This is what *frightens* us.'

'Yes, Lord,' I hear my father say.

I look at him; he looks at the sky.

'Permanus Lucien Dove was a hard man,' the preacher continues. 'We know he was, and we won't lie about it now. No, we won't. He was a hard, hard man. He was an angry man. But here in this part of Your earth, Lord, we know what it is that makes a black man hard. We know this. And this knowledge is what helps us *understand* Permanus Dove—what helps us pray here today that You, our Father, will find forgiveness for this man.'

Why, I wonder, is the preacher using so many words to describe something so simple, so final?

'He was an honest man,' he continues. 'He was a smart man. And he knew how to work. He knew how to work, Lord. He provided for his son, and for his grandson, and there's many good-hearted men who refuse even to do that. We know this, too. So as we stand here today, frightened and humble, we do ask You, Lord, to forgive Permanus Lucien Dove.'

Abruptly, as if impatient to get the whole affair over and done with, the preacher bends, grabbing a handful of the freshly dug dirt, then stands and says:

'This is all we are, Lord: dirt.'

He slowly sprinkles the black soil on the coffin.

'From dirt we arise,' he says, 'and to dirt we return. Amen, Lord. Amen.'

'Amen,' my father says.

He looks at me and nods his head, frowning.

'Amen,' I say.

'Well, men,' the preacher says, unbuttoning his shirt cuffs and rolling them up to his elbows, 'let's get busy.'

Quickly, then, and silently, the three of us begin to fill the sunlit grave with dirt.

'You're rather big to be a dancer,' she says. 'Aren't you? Are you sure you're not lying about that, too?'

I look at her and smile.

'You know, Maggie,' I say, 'I learnt a long time ago to let people think what they want. If they think I'm lying, then I let them go right on thinking it. Doesn't matter what I say; they're going to think it, anyway.'

'True,' she agrees, nodding her head and smiling. 'I believe you, though; don't worry.'

'I'm not worried,' I reply. 'I don't really care what you think. Not yet, anyway.'

She takes a sip of her fifth, or sixth, cup of tea and looks around the café.

We have been here for several hours, and as it is no longer raining, there are only a few customers left. The man behind the counter is washing dishes, an unlit cigarette dangling from his lips.

'I like you, Ulysses,' Maggie says, looking at me.

'I like you, too,' I reply.

She takes a cigarette from her purse and lights it.

'Do you want to be my boyfriend?' she asks.

She blows on the lit match, then tosses it on the floor and looks at me.

'Sure,' I reply, smiling. 'Why not?'

'*Why not*? You don't sound too enthusiastic about it.'

I shrug, watching her.

'Or worried.'

'Why should I be worried?' I ask.

'Well,' she replies, 'maybe I'm the one who's crazy.'
'I didn't know it was a contest.'
She giggles.
'Besides,' I say, winking at her, 'beautiful women are always crazy.
'Oh, really?' she groans. 'Is that supposed to be a compliment? I hate compliments.'
I smile.
'You know,' I say, 'Malcolm X believed that women, innately, couldn't be trusted; as proof he offered the fact that a woman who dislikes you will, when complimented on her appearance, begin to like you. That's all it takes.'
'Some women,' she says. 'But there's men like that, too. Besides, fuck Malcolm X.'
I look at her.
'He was just another man,' she says, 'travelling around the world while his wife stayed at home and did all the housework and looked after the kids.'
'Maybe she wanted to stay home and look after the kids. Have you ever thought of that?'
'Maybe she did. But I'll tell you this: if she didn't, it wouldn't matter. She'd still have to do it. There was no choice.'
She leans forward, resting her elbows on the table, and looks at me. Her tobacco-brown eyes are bright, searching.
'Hey,' she says, 'I love Malcolm. Honestly, I do. He was one of the brightest, most—most fascinating men to ever live. But he was still just a man.'
'That's not a bad thing, Maggie.'
'No,' she agrees, 'it isn't. But neither is it, in itself, a cause for celebration.'
'You've been reading *The Color Purple*, I see.'
She giggles, then says:
'Fuck you. And fuck Alice Walker. All I'm saying—regardless of whatever good qualities Malcolm had and inspired—is that his wife was still left at home to change diapers and scrub toi-

lets while he was touring France and Saudi Arabia and—and Egypt.'

'And who's still alive? Him or her?'

'Hey,' she says, 'we all have to die; death is no penalty.'

And so it goes. We sit, talking, for perhaps another hour, then decide to leave the Medina. As I am at the counter paying, I turn and see that Jonathan, or someone I presume is Jonathan, has entered the café. He is standing next to Maggie, talking.

Returning to the table, I extend my hand and introduce myself. He is younger, I think, than I had imagined: twenty-nine, thirty?

'Hey there,' I say. 'I'm Ulysses.'

His handshake is solid, strong.

'Hey, Ulysses,' he says. 'I'm Jonathan.'

He looks at Maggie.

'So,' he says, 'this is your partner in crime?'

Maggie looks up at me and smiles.

'Yes,' she replies. 'He kidnapped me last night in the hotel and dragged me to every wretched nightclub in Tangier.'

'I think it was Maggie who did the dragging,' I say, winking at Jonathan.

He is of average height and slender, with short, thick, black hair and strong, masculine features that are, I guess, either Jewish or Italian: full lips, prominent nose, brow, and jaw. He is wearing crisp, but faded blue jeans, leather, thick-soled sandals, and a white, long-sleeved, button-down shirt.

Cornell, I presume, or perhaps Princeton, but not Yale. Either way, I am certain, he is a Democrat.

'We were about to get something to eat,' I say to him. 'Of course you'll join us?'

He looks at Maggie; she smiles.

'Sure,' he replies, looking at me.

His teeth, I notice, are flawless.

We leave the café, waving at the waiter who grunts in return, and walk through the narrow, busy streets of the Medina.

As we walk, I am reminded of Mark Twain's description of Tangier: a crowded city of snowy tombs. Even when it is busy, crowded, I think, there is an almost eerie peace that suggests complete solitude, its noisy rhythms coalescing into a dirge.

Tangier, surely, is the loneliest place on earth.

Leaving the Medina, we walk downtown and find a small restaurant on the boulevard Mohammed V. Though we are the only patrons, we wait nearly an hour for our food: a large chicken tagine, which we share.

There is tension, I soon notice, between Maggie and Jonathan. Though the conversation is steady, lively, it is primarily between Jonathan and me, or Maggie and me, and rarely between the two of them. Occasionally, they look at each other, as if in silent acknowledgment of a shared secret, then look away.

Jonathan, I learn, is thirty-one years old. He is wealthy; he does not discuss the source. He was born and raised in Boston. He now lives in the Park Slope section of Brooklyn, but he travels extensively and is seldom there. He collects rare jazz, blues, and soul records. He is, indeed, a registered Democrat.

'And Maggie,' he says, smiling at her, 'I met in Paris, three years ago. She was working as a model and studying French.'

'I didn't know you were a model,' I say to Maggie.

In fact, I realize, I know even less about her than I do about him. Curiously, I do not want to know more.

'Well,' she says, shrugging, 'I wouldn't say I was a model. I did a couple runway shows and some print work, but that's about it. Seemed like the only black models who were getting any work were the ones who had Caucasian features and—and yellow skin.'

'White women with a tan,' I suggest.

'Amen,' she says, taking a drag of her cigarette.

'Yeah,' Jonathan adds, shaking his head. 'As a man of African descent, I find it especially frustrating that—'

'Oh, stop saying that,' Maggie suddenly, furiously, interrupts, setting her cigarette in the ashtray and looking up at the dark red ceiling.

'Stop saying what?' Jonathan asks, as if confused.

'That you're a man of African descent,' she replies, looking at me and shaking her head. 'You've said that before, and, really, it's pathetic, Jonathan.'

I look at him, studying his features.

'You're black?' I ask.

'No,' Maggie says. 'He is *not* black. He's Jewish. That's all. A Jew.'

'My great-grandmother,' he says, 'was about as—'

'Oh, just stop it,' Maggie interrupts again, nearly screaming. 'I am so sick of that story.'

Jonathan looks at her.

'What story?' he asks.

'How your great-great-grandmother was a slave named Tulip who lived to be a hundred and five,' she replies, angrily, 'with eleven children, all boys.'

'But it's true,' he says.

Though adamant, he is also, I can see, embarrassed, blushing.

'Well,' I say, 'I guess, technically, every last human being is of African descent. We all come from Africa, right?'

'Technically, yes,' Maggie says. 'But Jonathan's not being technical. He's not saying his ancestors were—'

'Don't speak for me, Maggie,' Jonathan interrupts. 'Alright? I can speak for myself.'

'He hates being Jewish,' Maggie says, looking at me. 'He hates being rich and bored and—and he thinks black people are having more fun than white people.'

Jonathan looks at her, silent.

'You want to be black,' I tell him, 'then go to Rwanda. Or go talk to Abner Louima. Then you can see how fun being black is in the real world.'

'I didn't say I was black, Maggie. I said I—'

'Oh, shut up,' she snaps. 'You are such a—'

I expect her to continue, but she surprises me by suddenly pushing back her chair and standing. Pulling her scarf up over her hair with the dramatic flair of an old movie actress, she takes her cigarette from the ashtray, inhales, and raises her head to look at Jonathan.

'Fuck you,' she says.

She snuffs out her cigarette in the ashtray.

'Good day,' she says, glaring at both of us. *'Brothers!'*

I watch as she steps away from the table, turns, and walks, or rather sashays, out of the small, shadowed restaurant.

The two of us turn and look at one another.

'She's crazy,' Jonathan says, still blushing.

I am silent, for a moment, then say:

'Good.'

'Spontaneous combustion: the process of catching fire as a result of heat generated by internal chemical action.'

I move my index finger to the next entry:

'Spontaneous generation: the theory, now discredited, that living organisms can originate in nonliving matter independently of other living matter; abiogenesis.'

I flip to the beginning of the dictionary, page three, and move my finger down the left-hand column.

'Abiogenesis,' I whisper. 'Greek origin. Abio. Lifeless. Plus Genesis. Spontaneous generation.'

I look away, thinking, then look again at the opened book before me. Sliding my finger directly parallel from page three to page two, I stop at the right-hand column.

'Abednego: one of three captives who came out of the fiery furnace unharmed. Daniel 3:12-27.'

I set down the dictionary, looking at the shadowed row of reference books on my desk. Shifting the lampshade, I lean forward and, finding the Bible, take it and open it. Flipping through the thin, gilded pages, I stop, suddenly, and look behind me.

In the doorway to my bedroom, shirtless, is my father.

'What are you doing in the dark, boy?' he asks.

His voice is soft and deep, as if tired.

'Homework,' I lie, pointing to the books in front of me.

He stands, looking at me for a moment, then says:

'You don't want to wreck your eyes, Ulysses. Is that lamp enough light to be reading by?'

Just leave me alone, I want to say.

'Yes, sir,' I answer.

'Well, alright, then,' he says, after a moment's silence. 'I guess I'll see you in the morning.'

'Okay. Goodnight, Dad.'

He does not move; he stands, staring.

'Is everything okay, Dad?'

'Just do your homework, boy,' he says, turning slowly and walking down the darkened hallway. I hear his bedroom door open, then close.

'Motherfucker,' I whisper, turning back to the opened Bible.

I flip to the book of Daniel and read, quickly, chapter three.

'Shadrach, Meschach, Abednego,' I say when done, setting the Bible atop the dictionary.

I look again through my doorway and down the darkened hallway.

There are people, I think, who can spontaneously combust, who have spontaneously combusted; this fascinates me. What, I wonder, would such an event look like? A spark from the eye or ear, perhaps a puff of smoke, and then—fire?

I turn to the desk, adjusting the lampshade until a perfect circle of yellow light is formed on its surface. In the center of this circle, I place my left hand, palm down; looking at it, I whisper:

'Burn.'

Later that night as I am doing push-ups in my hotel room, there is a knock at the door. Irritated at the interruption, I continue my exercises and yell:

'What?'

'Hey, Ulysses,' I hear Jonathan reply. 'It's me, Jonathan. You busy?'

'Yes,' I reply, 'I am.'

Silence.

'Well,' he eventually says, 'when you're done with whatever—whatever it is you're doing, why don't you—'

I quickly stand and open the door.

'Oh, hey,' Jonathan says, looking first at my bare chest, then at my face.

'Don't worry,' I say, catching my breath. 'I wasn't jacking off; I was just doing push-ups.'

He laughs. I smile.

'Anyway,' he says, 'Maggie sent me over to ask if you wanted to go to a party.'

'A party?' I ask, turning and walking to the bed.

I take a towel and wipe the back of my neck and under my arms.

'Yeah,' he says. 'I guess James Brown is having a party at his place tonight. Maggie met him today after—after she left the restaurant.'

'James Brown, huh?' I say, turning around and looking at Jonathan. 'I didn't know he had a place in Tangier.'

'Neither did I, but I guess he does,' Jonathan replies. 'Somewhere over by the Casbah.'

'Well,' I say, 'I couldn't exactly miss a party at the Godfather's, now, could I?'

I wipe my chest, then toss the towel back on the bed.

'I hear you, brother,' Jonathan says.

I look at him and frown.

'Well, you tell Maggie to come and get me when she's ready,' I say.

'She's ready now,' he replies.

'Now?'

'That's right.'

'Well, give me a few minutes; I'll meet you guys in the lobby.'

'Okay, then,' he says, reaching forward and shutting the door.

Not having time to go downstairs and shower, I wash up in the small sink, rub a little patchouli and coconut oil under my arms, then slip on a clean black shirt and cotton trousers. I put on my yellow babouches, check myself out in the small, cracked mirror above the sink, and then leave the room.

By the time we get to the party, having smoked a joint along the way, the three of us are stoned, or, as Maggie says, fucking fucked up. Either way, I am, indeed, high.

It is a huge apartment, modern, completely white—white walls, white rugs, white furniture and ceiling, white baby grand piano. Huge French doors lead onto a stone terrace, painted white, with a view that stretches, to the east, across the twinkling lights of Tangier and, to the west, out onto the Mediterranean Sea.

In the center of the main room, several couples dance, glasses in their hands. Elsewhere, countless men and women are sitting, standing, talking, laughing; of all these people, Maggie and I included, only five or six are not of European descent.

'Pretty vanilla crowd for James Brown,' I whisper to Maggie, who is smoking a cigarette and looking apathetically around the crowded room.

'James Brown,' she replies, looking at me. 'Is James Brown here?'

'It's his party, isn't it?' I ask.

'I don't think so,' she replies. 'Where'd you hear that?'

I search the room for Jonathan but, unable to locate him, I look at Maggie and say:

'Jonathan said that you met James Brown today and he invited you to a party.'

She looks at me, no longer smiling.

'That asshole,' she says, taking a drag of her cigarette. 'He is such a fucking liar; just wait 'til I see him.'

I shake my head and laugh softly.

'You two are crazy,' I remark.

She looks up at me, frowning.

'Well,' she responds, 'if that isn't the snowflake calling the snowball white.'

She turns and abruptly walks through the mill of people and out onto the terrace. I watch, wondering what has happened, and briefly entertain the notion of following her. Instead, I look around the room and wonder, Well, whose party is this, then?

In the kitchen, mixing drinks, is a bartender named Habib. I ask him for vodka and grapefruit juice, no ice. He passes me my drink, and I wander, glass in hand, from room to room.

My mind, like a top, spins and spins, then slows until it finally stops. Just as quickly, it begins again to spin and spin, then slow, then stop. The process is endless, and not unpleasant.

I meet an Egyptian woman, now living in Paris, named Marci. She is short, olive-skinned, and voluptuous, with a flat, homely face and wild, curly brown hair. She is, she says, an African dancer.

'These Moroccan men,' she opines, 'they're pigs. I can barely get down the street without being called a prostitute, or at least treated like one.'

I look at her huge, sagging breasts, barely concealed beneath a flimsy, red tank top, and say:

'Maybe if you didn't dress like one.'

She looks up at me, eyes narrowed, whispering in Arabic, then quickly walks away.

I take a gulp of my drink and look around. The crowd, it seems, is getting larger, noisier. People are laughing, drinking, talking, dancing; the music, I think, is much too loud.

The overhead lights have been dimmed, I notice, and huge, red candles have been lit. The room is now a shimmering haze of shadow, smoke, and tiny glimmers of candle fire. Once again, I wonder, whose party is this?

Still I spin.

I meet two American students, Janice and Khadijah, who are in Morocco for a three-month university exchange program.

Khadijah is fat, of Arabian descent, with the beautiful face and eager, hopeful manner typical of fat girls. Janice is blond, healthy, and harmlessly rebellious; she rolls her own cigarettes and, so she says, loves an African-American boy majoring in corporate law.

'Who I feel sorry for,' she explains, plucking a piece of tobacco from her bottom lip, 'are the women who clean our hotel room. Have you seen how they work? God. They don't even have mops; they get down on their knees and use a rag! It's just heartbreaking.'

'I know,' Khadijah agrees, smiling sadly. 'I asked one of them how much she was paid, and she wouldn't tell me. I told her I'd give her five dollars if she told me—but she wouldn't. Too ashamed, I guess.'

Still I spin.

Across the room, I see Jonathan talking with a tall, bald-headed white man; they are laughing. I look out onto the terrace, expecting to see Maggie, but I am drawn only to the sky's hazy, blue darkness.

I meet a thin, blond Austrian man named Wolfgang who tells me he is dying of leukemia. He has, he says, three months to live. Intrigued, I question him further until he interrupts me:

'Please, I don't want to talk about it.'

Finishing my drink, I return to the kitchen for a second, thanking Habib, and make my way to the terrace. In one corner, talking softly, are Janice and Khadijah; they see me, smile, and quickly return to the party.

In the western corner, alone, stands Maggie; she leans against the stone balcony and looks out into the darkness. A light, warm breeze flutters the hem of her long, purple, blue-spangle-trimmed skirt. She is smoking a cigarette.

'Hey, stranger,' I say.

She turns, looks at me, and smiles.

'How are you doing, big boy?' she asks, turning away to look again into the dark blue sky.

'I'm alright,' I reply, standing next to her. 'How are you? Still fucking fucked up?'

'Maybe just a bit,' she replies, giggling.

She leans over the balcony, looking below at the huge stone wall that separates the rocky shore and the tide from the Medina's narrow, crumbling streets.

'Have you seen Jonathan?' I ask.

'For a minute,' she replies, looking up, 'but I told him to fuck off. Fucking cocksucker.'

I smile but say nothing.

'Did you know,' she asks, 'that men who get fucked up the ass will be condemned in the next life to wash their faces with the urine of Jews, forever?'

'No,' I reply, laughing, 'I didn't know that.'

'Well,' she says, taking a long, slow drag of her cigarette, 'I was talking with some guy earlier, a Jew, of course, and that's what he said. Why he would tell me such a thing, I don't know. But it's the law, he said. Islamic law.'

'Oh, really,' I say. 'I've never heard any such thing. It sounds more like a fantasy to me.'

She lowers her head suddenly, rubbing her eyes with her fists, like a tired child, then looks up, red-eyed, and asks:

'Have you ever been to Spain?'

'No,' I reply. 'But I kind of like the music.'

She giggles.

'You so crazy,' she says.

'Hey,' I say. 'Didn't you just get mad at me for calling you and Jonathan crazy?'

'Dogs get mad,' she replies, winking at me. 'Humans get angry. Besides, I wasn't angry; I just wanted to come out here on the terrace.'

'Okay,' I say. 'Whatever.'

'You're so sensitive,' she says, smiling. 'I feel like I have to—'

'You're a beautiful woman,' I interrupt, stepping toward her. 'Do you know that?'

'Yes,' she replies, stepping away from me. 'I do.'

'Where are you going?' I ask.

'Where are *you* going?' she replies. 'You weren't going to kiss me, were you?'

I smile and say:

'I was thinking about it.'

'Well,' she replies, 'I'd rather have your cock in my mouth.'

I look at her, saying nothing.

'Just kidding,' she says, laughing.

She stops, abruptly looks at me, and then laughs again.

'Oh, boy,' she says, 'if you could see your face.'

'Very funny,' I say.

'I'm sorry, sweetie,' she says, putting her hand on my shoulder. 'Come here and kiss me, then.'

She pulls me toward her.

'Well,' I say, 'now that you've completely destroyed the mood.'

I set my glass on the stone ledge, and raising my hand to her chin, I kiss her; she tastes, I think, like butterscotch.

Looking into her brown eyes, I ask:

'What have you been drinking? You taste sweet.'

'Piss,' she replies, pulling away from me. 'I've been drinking piss.'

I watch as she takes a cigarette from her purse and lights it.

'You know,' I say, suddenly irritated, 'these little jokes of yours can be—'

'Sorry,' she interrupts, taking a drag of her cigarette. 'It's just, well, I hate all that stuff—it's gross.'

'*Gross?* Well, thank you very much.'

'Oh, calm down,' she says. 'It's not you. I just—I don't know—I just feel like laughing or—or throwing up when I hear men say things like that.'

'Like what?' I ask.

'*You taste so sweet.* I mean, give me a break. What is this, a Terry McMillan novel?'

'I don't think I should have to defend myself,' I say. 'But you *do* taste sweet. Like butterscotch. It wasn't a line, Maggie.'

'Oh, please; it's all a line.'

'Hey,' I say, shrugging, 'I just wanted to kiss you; that's all. I haven't played you even once since last night; so what all this bullshit is about, I don't know. Damn, it's not like I tried to shove your head in my lap.'

'Now you're mad,' she says, frowning childishly.

'Dogs get mad,' I say. 'Remember? And humans get—'

'Exactly,' she interrupts, smiling.

I shake my head, wondering, who is this woman?

'Come on,' she says, taking my arm. 'Let's go back into the party. I need to find Jonathan and beat him up; you're too tough for me, brotherman.'

The mare turns her head, slowly, looking up at my father as he kneels next to her.

'It's okay, girl,' he whispers, gently stroking her sweaty, black flank.

She looks at him and then looks away. She bows her head and nibbles gingerly at the damp straw that covers the stall's floor.

'You just don't care about nothing,' he whispers. 'Hey, girl?'

Continuing to stroke her, he turns and looks back into the warm, dusty darkness of the barn. Next to the stall's opened gate sits the dog, watching, its ears raised as if in alarm. My father looks at the mongrel, past it, his expression blank, set. A fat, black horsefly buzzes lazily about his face, and he swats it away absentmindedly.

He turns, looking down at the mare.

'Girl,' he says, 'what am I going to do with you?'

She continues to nibble at the straw, her legs curled awkwardly beneath her swollen belly. From her vagina protrudes the still, brown leg of her foal.

'You don't even know you're pregnant,' he says, 'do you?'

The horse looks at him and, again, looks away.

'Well, okay, then,' he says, as if in reply.

I kneel, resting my hands on the dusty, wooden floor, and peer over the edge of the loft.

Slowly, still crouching, my father unbuttons and takes off his shirt and then throws it, without looking, next to the dog. His huge, muscled chest rises, falls. Biting his lower lip, he rests on the stall's floor, shifts to his left hip, and moves next to the mare's haunches.

'Now, you just be good,' he says softly, his bare back resting against the side of the stall. 'You hear me, girl?' he adds, looking down at the mare.

Slowly, gently, he takes hold of her foal's leg; it does not move. Carefully, he slides his hand along the thin, bony leg and then into the mare, up to his wrist.

Is it a colt, I wonder, or a filly?

The mare, as if unaware of him, continues nibbling at the straw.

'That's right, girl,' my father whispers. 'You just be good.'

From behind him comes the sound of the dog whimpering, growling. My father turns, looking at the dog, and whispers angrily:

'You be quiet.'

The dog becomes silent.

My father begins to push his hand deeper inside the mare until, finally, his bare shoulder rests against the underside of her thick, black tail.

Is he looking for something? I wonder. If so, what? Though I have seen him, and my grandfather, do this before, there is an unfamiliar calmness, a gentility, to my father, and to the horse, that frightens me. Something, I know, is *different*.

With his hand, he begins to shift the foal, to turn it around, within its mother's womb; perhaps, I think, it is trapped somehow. His face next to the mare's flank, he stares intently, his eyes narrowed, at her slick, black hide.

He begins to slowly slide his arm out of the horse's vagina.

Suddenly, startling me, the foal begins to exit its mother's womb. My father leans back, as if frightened. I stare for a moment at his bloodied arm, and then watch as the foal slips with ease from its mother onto the mucky straw floor.

'Jesus H. Christ,' I hear my father say.

Is he afraid, I wonder, or angry?

The mare turns, her ears back, and begins neighing, her huge head rising, falling, in a rapid, jerking motion. My father, using the stall's side for support, struggles quickly to his feet and steps back.

The foal, I realize, is deformed, its huge head twisted, misshapen. The right hind leg is missing.

'It's okay, girl,' my father says. 'It's okay.'

I watch, mesmerized, as the placenta and the uterus gush, dark and thick, slimy, from the mare's vagina. The foal, I notice, is not moving, and I know that if it is not yet dead, it soon will be.

The mare kicks her legs out and struggles weakly to her feet, the dark, thick blood continuing to gush from her vagina, down her legs, and onto the stall's straw-covered floor.

Her head rising, falling, swinging from left to right, right to left, she begins to frantically stamp her front hooves, neighing loudly, kicking with her hind legs against the stall's wooden side and bringing them down onto the soft, lifeless body of her offspring.

My father turns quickly, stepping out of the stall, and closes the gate behind him. The dog leaps up to the gate, barking, whimpering, and my father angrily kicks it away.

'You get out of here!' he yells.

The dog turns, shifting back with its tail between its legs, but does not leave. Looking up at the gate, it continues to whimper.

My father stands, his hands on the smooth wooden gate, and watches as the mare continues to stamp and kick, lowering and raising her huge neck.

'C'mon, girl,' he says, as if to himself. 'You be good; you be quiet.'

Once again, the dog leaps to the gate, and my father turns and kicks it in the ribs, yelling:

'Goddamn!'

The dog falls, then rises and runs, howling, through the narrowly opened barn door into the yellow haze of sunlight.

My father turns to the mare, watching in silence as her movements slow.

'You lay down, girl,' he says softly. 'Go on.'

Her head falls but this time does not rise.

The blood continues to gush, thicker now, darker, almost black, from her vagina. She stamps her front hooves slowly, swings her head to the left, her nose just inches from the ground, and looks at the lifeless, bloodied form of her foal. With her right hind hoof, she kicks at it lazily, pushing it into the corner of the stall. It is, I realize, a colt.

My father watches in silence, his hands clenched tightly across the top of the gate.

The mare's front legs buckle beneath her and she falls forward to her knees, her head smashing sideways against the stall's side.

She remains still for a moment, breathing deeply, her muscled haunches raised until finally her hind legs buckle as well and she falls, with a heavy thump, to the stall's floor.

She raises her huge head, slowly, then rests it. Still she bleeds.

'I'm sorry, girl,' my father whispers.

I watch the slow, then slower, rise and fall of the horse's belly.

'There was nothing I could do,' my father says. 'There was just—'

He turns and walks quickly out of the barn into the hot afternoon sun. Behind him, the dog slinks back into the barn and trots quickly to the stall door. Sniffing about, it scratches lazily at the dirt and begins, again, to whimper.

By now, we are no longer high; we are, however, drunk. Maggie sits on the edge of the bed, smiling at me, and lets her sandals fall to the floor. I turn off the light and walk to the bed.

'This room is awful,' she says. 'It's like being in a Depression-era hospital. You should see our room; it has a terrace and high ceilings, a private bathroom. Except the walls are white, and white walls depress me.'

I put my finger to her lips and whisper:
'Shut up.'

As I reach for her shoulders, she pulls away from me, falling back across the bed, and holds her arms up, out. From outside the opened window, we hear the sudden cry of what sounds like a cat, fighting.

'Is that a baby?' she asks, craning her neck and looking out the window.

'I think it's a cat,' I reply.

'Oh, God,' she says, hugging herself. 'Could you shut the window, please? It gives me the creeps.'

I do as she asks, then return to the side of the bed and begin to unbutton my shirt. She sits up, resting on her elbows, and watches me, I notice briefly, as if she were a politician and I, her whore.

Though the room is dark, a shaft of light from beneath the door illuminates me as I slowly undress, then stand, naked, looking at her.

'Your turn,' I say, holding my erection in my hand.

'Where'd you get that scar?' she asks, looking at the thick, smooth scar beneath my belly button.

'In the war,' I reply.

'Which one?' she asks, giggling.

'The one inside of me,' I answer.

She rolls her eyes.

'Can you dance for me?' she asks, not moving.

'Are you serious?' I ask. 'Or is this another of your jokes?'

'My jokes? You're the one with the jokes, mister.'

I say nothing, watching her.

'I'm serious,' she replies. 'I want you to dance for me.'

'Well,' I say. 'I don't know if I can dance with—with this.'

I hold my hard cock and, gently, shake it.

'Try,' she says.

I expect her to smile, but she does not.

'Come on,' she insists. 'Dance.'

I look at her; arching my back, then standing straight, I extend my left leg into an arabesque. She smiles. Bringing my leg first forward, then into a developpe, and finally into a turnout, I stop, still looking at her, and execute a quick plie and then, rising, a fouetté.

My cock still erect, I stand, wobbling slightly, and look at her.

'That's a fouetté,' I say. 'It's normally for women but I—I figured I'd give you a treat.'

She says nothing for a moment, then smiles softly and replies:

'Well, thank you kindly. But is that all you do? Ballet? You don't do anything more—more modern?'

I look down at my erection, which is beginning to soften, and say:

'Yeah, I do something more modern. Let me show you.'

She opens her mouth as if to say something sarcastic, then stops.

I move toward the bed and, taking her by the arm, gently pull her to her feet. With the head of my cock pushed up against her belly, I raise her arms, slowly, and slip off her top. She does not resist. I bend down and slowly undo her skirt, letting it fall to the floor.

She is not wearing panties. I lean forward, kissing her gently below her belly button; she shivers, putting her hands on my bare shoulders. I stand, kissing her as I rise, and look at her face. She closes her eyes and leans forward, resting her head against my chest.

'You have no hair on your body,' I hear her whisper, as she lightly traces her hands down my back and across my ass.

'Neither do you,' I reply, putting my hands on her hips and beginning to rub gently up against her firm belly.

'You're just saying that,' she replies, giggling, 'because you like me.'

'Maybe,' I whisper, kissing her neck, her jaw.

She lowers her hands, sliding them across and around my thighs. With one hand, she lightly cups my balls; with the other, she grips my cock.

'That tickles,' I say.
'Does this?' she asks, squeezing both her hands, tightly.
'No,' I reply, wincing. 'That hurts.'
'Good,' she says, squeezing even tighter.

It is a cold, windy afternoon as I take the hay bales from the back of the pickup truck and stack them in the barn. I move quickly, arranging them neatly in rows of three and stacks of five; I will soon be done.

With perhaps seven bales left to stack, I watch as my father walks into the barn and stands next to the truck. He is wearing his overalls, a red kerchief around his thick neck, and an old, sweat-stained cap. His face is dusty, with a smear of dirt or oil across his brow. I look at him and think, I hate you.

'What are you doing?' he asks, taking off his cap and scratching the back of his head.

I look at the stack of bales behind me and the ones remaining in the truck, then say:

'What does it look like? I'm stacking the bales.'

'I know you're stacking the bales, smartass,' he replies, putting back on his cap. 'Why are you stacking them so close to the door? I told you to put them in the back, next to the last stall there.'

I slide another bale off the back of the truck and put it atop the stack.

'It's easier for me to get to them here,' I reply. 'And they're not in the way. So what does it matter?'

He steps closer to the truck.

'It matters,' he says, looking at me, 'because I say it matters. Now, I want you to move them where I told you to put them in the first place.'

I look at him and, again, I think, I hate you.

'You can't be serious,' I say. 'I'm almost done!'

'Well, maybe this'll teach you to listen to me,' he replies. 'Now, go on; get busy.'

I look down at the dust and loose hay at the bottom of the nearly empty pickup.

'No,' I say, looking up at my father, who has already turned to leave.

He stops and turns around.

'What did you say?' he asks, looking at me.

'I said, no.'

He opens his mouth, slightly. After a moment of silence, he says: 'Are you sure you want to do this, boy?'

I look at him, not sure what he means. The muscles in my stomach begin to tighten; immediately, I am frightened.

'I just don't see what the big deal is,' I reply, looking slightly to the left of his face. 'If I'm the one who has to—'

Suddenly, as if by magic, he is next to me.

'Alright,' I begin to say. 'I'll do it the—'

With one hand, he holds me, pushing me back up against the side of the stall; with the other, he punches me in the face, breaking my nose.

Later that night, looking at my bruised and swollen face, my grandfather says:

'You were too pretty, anyway, boy.'

Maggie and I are in bed, sleeping, when I am awakened by a knock at the door. My eyes still closed, I turn my head toward the door and yell:

'Who is it?'

'Is Maggie in there?' I hear Jonathan ask. He sounds upset.

'Yes,' I reply. 'And she's sleeping.'

I open my eyes and look at her; she is awake, staring up at the ceiling. Like a corpse in a coffin, she lies perfectly straight, still, her hands folded on her stomach.

'Good morning,' I whisper, kissing her lightly on the cheek. She remains silent, not moving. Is she angry? I wonder.

'Well, wake her up,' I hear Jonathan demand. 'I need to talk to her.'

Suddenly, Maggie sits straight and yells:

'What do you want, Jonathan?'

There is silence, as she turns and looks at me.

'Good morning, heartache,' she whispers, smiling.

'I need to talk to you!' I hear Jonathan yell.

Shaking her head, Maggie throws the blankets off, gets out of bed, and, surprising me, walks naked to the door and opens it. In the light of day, I notice, her body is flawless, a fine, brown frame.

'What do you want?' she screams.

Jonathan stands in the doorway, his hands in his pockets, and looks at her, at me, and again at her.

'Jesus, Maggie,' he says, 'put some clothes on.'

'Oh, fuck off,' Maggie replies. 'You've seen me naked before. Now, what do you want?'

He's seen her naked, I think.

Suddenly, Jonathan seems embarrassed; he looks down at the floor, then up. On the verge of saying something, he glances at me, then at Maggie, and still remains silent.

'Oh, brother,' Maggie groans. 'What are you? Shy? Just go back to the room; I'll meet you there in five minutes. Okay?'

Jonathan nods his head, and Maggie slams the door, turning to look at me.

'What was that?' I ask, sitting straight.

'It's a long, boring story,' she replies. 'Maybe one day you can read the book.'

She walks to the bed, sits, and begins to dress.

'Hey,' I say, touching her lightly on the shoulder, 'look at this.'

As she turns her head, I pull the blanket from my lap and hold my erection in my hand.

'Yeah, I know,' she says, turning away. 'I've seen it before.'

'Oh, okay,' I reply, laughing softly. 'So that's how it is this morning.'

She becomes still, then giggles softly and says:

'Don't worry, sailor; I'll be back for more. But I have to go—go deal with that asshole first.'

'You two aren't a couple,' I ask, pulling the blanket back across my lap, 'are you?'

She stands, pulling up her skirt, and faces me.

'Get real,' she says. 'Do you think I'd be over here with you if Jonathan and I were a couple? I already told you: he's *not* my boyfriend.'

'Well, he sure acts like he is,' I reply. 'Not that I care, really; I'm just curious.'

She slips on her top.

'No,' she says. 'You wouldn't care, would you?'

She bends, picking up her purse, and walks to the sink. She pulls back her hair and ties it in a lazy twist at the nape of her neck; with a leather barrette from her purse, she fastens it. Bending forward, she turns on the tap and begins splashing water on her face and neck.

I get out of bed, slip on my pants, and walk to the window, opening it. The day is bright and sunny, and the narrow streets and Petit Socco are bustling with people, with noise. I am startled by the call for prayer as it crackles, then booms, from a loudspeaker somewhere on the other side of the building across from me.

'*Allahu Akbar,*' the deep, strong voice calls. '*Allahu Akbar.*'

I turn, looking at the small travel clock on the table next to the bed; it is nearly noon.

'*Allahu Akbar. Allahu Akbar.*'

Maggie shuts off the water, pats her face dry with my towel, and turns toward me. Looking fresh and well rested, she smiles.

'I'm going to get a coffee with Jonathan,' she says, brushing a loose, wet strand of hair behind her ear. 'See what crawled up his ass. What are you going to do?'

'I don't know,' I reply. 'Maybe go take a shower.'

'Well, I'll leave our door open; if you want, you can have a shower there. Better than that rat trap downstairs.'

'Sure,' I say, envisioning the downstairs shower. With neither a towel rack nor a shower spigot, it is really only a small, tiled room with a water tap and a rusted drain in the center of the floor.

'Give me a few minutes,' she says, walking toward me.

Putting her hand in the center of my chest, she kisses me.

'No problem,' I say, watching as she grabs her purse, returns to the side of the bed, slips on her sandals, then walks to the door. Opening it, she looks over her shoulder at me.

'Thanks, sailor,' she says, winking. 'Wait here 'til I get back. Okay? We'll do something.'

I nod my head, watching as she leaves the room, closing the door slowly, quietly, behind her.

Listening to the sounds outside my window, I walk to the bed and pull back the thick, dark blue blanket; the sheets are still clean. I make the bed, neatly folding the corners and smoothing its surface.

Once done, I do fifty push-ups and fifty sit-ups. While doing them, I think of Maggie, of our night together, and I soon get an erection. I think of Maggie and Jonathan together, and my erection softens.

There are two subjects worthy of a serious mind, Yeats once wrote: sex and death. Finished with my exercises, I stretch back on the cool, brown-tiled floor and look up at the ceiling. He was wrong, I think. It is not sex and death that are worthy of a serious mind; it is what we do to achieve or to avoid them.

Although I'm tired, I sit up and then stand. I grab my towel and shaving kit, then leave the room, locking the door behind me. Barefoot, shirtless, I walk quickly down the hallway; I open Maggie's and Jonathan's door and, once inside, close it behind me.

The room, just as Maggie said, is huge and bright, with two queen-sized beds, high, white walls, and French doors that open onto a small terrace overlooking the Petit Socco. Cursing Abderahim, I quickly enter the washroom and undress, setting my towel and shaving kit on the closed toilet lid.

Hoping to be finished and out of the room by the time Maggie and Jonathan return, I shower quickly, brushing my teeth and cleaning my nails beneath the rush of lukewarm water. As I am washing my hair, I hear a man say:

'*Bonjour.* Hello?'

Startled, I turn, pulling the transparent shower curtain back, and see Abderahim standing in the doorway, looking at me. His dark, bearded face is stiff, angry.

'Oh, hey, Abderahim,' I say. 'I thought it was, well, Miss—Maggie, the woman who's staying here, said it was okay. I'll just be a minute.'

I release the shower curtain, stepping back beneath the water, and rinse the shampoo from my hair. Looking up, I see that Abderahim is still standing, watching me.

'Damn, brother,' I say, 'give me a little privacy.'

He steps forward and pulls back the shower curtain. Staring above my head, he says:

'Sir, this isn't your room.'

I look at him, shaking my head, and shut off the water. Pushing him aside, I step out of the shower and grab my towel.

'I'm going to tell you this one more time,' I say, drying myself. 'The woman who is staying in this room said I could use her shower. Okay? She and her friend went for a coffee; when they get back, you can ask them.'

'There is no woman in this room,' Abderahim replies, looking at me. 'There is *no one* in this room, sir. Except, of course, for you.'

Standing straight, I look at him, then around the room. There is, I realize, no indication, no evidence, that it has been used by anyone but myself.

Wrapping the towel around my waist, I walk quickly into the bedroom. There is no luggage, no trash, no old newspaper, no folded map. The beds are perfectly made. I look out the opened French doors, then back at Abderahim; he is frowning, his arms folded, and slowly shaking his head.

'Oh, Lord,' I say, looking up at the ceiling and laughing softly. 'This must be the wrong room. I am so sorry, Abderahim.'

He looks at me, still silent.

'I don't know why,' I say, 'but I thought this was their room. My apologies.'

'Whose room?' he asks.

'Maggie and—and Jonathan,' I reply, returning to the bathroom. 'You know, the American black woman and her—her *ami jouife.*'

'There are no such people in this hotel,' I hear him say.

Rolling the towel and my dirty trousers into a bundle, I grab my soap, shampoo, and shaving kit, and return to the bedroom.

'I know,' I reply, looking at him. 'They're having a coffee, but they'll be back soon; don't worry.'

He looks at me, his face empty of expression.

'There are no such people in this hotel,' he repeats. 'As of this morning, we have seven guests: you, a German couple, a Canadian couple, a gentleman from St. Vincent, and a lady from Australia. There are no—'

'I've seen you talking with them,' I interrupt. 'More than once. I've seen you.'

'No, sir,' he says. 'You haven't.'

'Yes,' I insist, 'I have. I'm not imagining it.'

'Perhaps you have seen me talking with other guests,' he says, calmly. 'And mistaken them for—for your friends.'

I look at him, searching his placid face.

'If you need to use a shower in the future, sir,' he says, 'tell me, and I will give you—'

'Did Maggie put you up to this?' I ask, interrupting him. 'That crazy—'

'Please, sir,' he says, motioning with his hand toward the opened door. I look at the door, then back at him.

I turn, holding my belongings, then rush out of the room, down the hallway, and, fumbling for my key, open the door. I throw my stuff on the bed, shut the door, and stand, breathing deeply. I close my eyes.

'That crazy bitch,' I whisper.

Unable to see either of the needles, I move my hand gently across the dark purple bedspread; finding one, I hold it between my thumb and forefinger.

Where, I wonder, is my father?

Looking up, I see that the bedroom door is securely shut and locked. Still I am nervous.

Hunching over, I pinch the loose folds of my foreskin, then pull it outward, stretching it tightly until it begins, almost, to hurt. Taking the needle, I put its tip lightly against the underside of the taut, dark brown skin, then hold it there.

Inhaling, then slowly exhaling, I push the needle upwards, causing a slight, sharp rise in the foreskin. I close my eyes, for a moment, then open them.

Inhaling again, then exhaling, I quickly push the needle through the skin. Surprisingly, there is no blood.

The inside of my thighs begin to tremble as I slowly push the needle. When it is halfway through, I stop. I sit, fascinated, looking at the needle's tip, and slowly let go of my foreskin.

With my right hand, I continue to hold the shaft of my cock as it quickly, steadily, becomes erect.

I look up at the door, listening, then again look down.

As my cock hardens, and the foreskin retracts, the needle begins to twist sideways, causing the skin to pinch and bleed slightly. I let go of my cock, clenching the bed on either side of me, then whisper:

'Ouch.'

My cock fully erect, the needle now rests tightly against the side of my shaft. As if malformed, the foreskin curves, in a thick fold, rising from the middle of the shaft on one side, to just below the glans on the other.

Using my thumb and middle finger, I touch both ends of the needle and, like a dial, begin to gently turn it clockwise. There is a sudden, sharp pain, almost unbearable. I stop, then take a deep breath.

Again, I begin to turn the needle; again, just as suddenly, I stop.

Searching for the second needle, I slide my hand across the bed. Finding it, I take it and gently run its tip along the length of my shaft, stopping at the rounded curve of the head.

Mesmerized, I stare at the exact point where the needle touches my flesh.

Can I do it? I wonder, gently pushing the needle.

I close my eyes, breathing deeply, and begin to push the needle into the swollen head of my cock. Abruptly, I stop.

I can't do it, I realize, opening my eyes.

Angry, I take the needle and, looking up at the bedroom door, push it deep into my left thigh. Stifling a scream, I double over and instantly, unexpectedly, ejaculate onto my belly.

By the next morning, I am sick. I lie in bed atop the blanket, unable to move, and stare at the ceiling. My mind spins, wobbles; the room turns. Occasionally, I am able to sleep but not for long; I drift in and out from dream to reality to dream—which is which no longer matters.

I dream of Maggie: she returns, admitting her prank, and we make love while Jonathan watches, crying. I dream of Jonathan, alone: he tells me that Maggie has returned to America. I dream of my father and grandfather, unable to distinguish one from the other. I dream of dandelions.

I try to focus, to stay awake. I try to move, to rise, but I am unable to do so. Determined to remain lucid, I count to a hundred, in French. I fall asleep. I awake, reciting the alphabet, first in English, then in Greek. Again, I fall asleep. I awake, barely able to grab the water bottle on the nightstand and take a sip.

I imagine a dance; I am dancing. In the gymnasium of a small town's high school, I dance, alone, with neither music, nor audience. I bend, then bow, turn, twist, jump; I soar. I fall to my knees, then rise, then fall, then rise. I jump. I call my name.

I open my eyes. Leaning over the side of the bed, I vomit. Remaining still, I close my eyes, then vomit again.

'That bitch has a Jew dick up her pussy one night,' I hear my grandfather say, 'and the next night she has yours; doesn't that *frost* you, boy? Doesn't that just get you?'

I look up; he is standing next to the window, leaning against the wall, his arms folded across his chest.

'They're friends,' I say. 'They're just—they're just friends.'

'Hell,' he says, laughing, 'they ain't even real.'

Bending forward, he slaps his knees and laughs. Still laughing, he looks up and says:

'Son?'

He stops laughing.

I close my eyes, pulling myself, pushing myself, back up against the damp, flat pillow. For a moment, I am no longer sick; I feel fine, rested. I take a deep breath, as if at the end of a long race, and, once again, the room begins to spin. Trapped at the center, I clench the blanket and wait for the spinning to stop.

'Murderer!' a woman screams, her voice rising as if from the bottom of a well, echoing, bounding, rebounding, reverberating again and again.

'Murderer.'

Then, in a whisper:

'I saw it, baby; I saw it all. You strangled him with your bare hands; then you took him and you buried him. You did it, baby; admit it. Just—just say it, nigger. Say it.'

'No,' I murmur.

'And you don't even care enough to think about it. It's just mud to you. Just muck. Gone. Telling people like—just muck.'

'No,' I repeat.

There is a knock at the door. I watch as Abderahim enters, carrying a steaming bowl of what I presume to be soup. He sets it on the nightstand and looks at me. He is obviously disgusted. Or is he?

'Eat this,' he says softly. 'It will make you feel better.'

I look at him but say nothing.

'I'm going to the mosque,' he says. 'I'll come to see you when I get back.'

He touches the back of his hand to my forehead.

Still I am silent.

'Sleep, brother,' he says. 'Sleep.'
When he is gone, as if in obedience, I sleep.

'What we want,' he says, 'is someone to blame. Like we'd be different people if this person or that person hadn't done what they did. Like everything would be better if only it was different. Like movie stars aren't fucked up and rich people always love their kids. And like kids who are loved don't get—don't get abused.'

What, I wonder, is he talking about?

'It's all the same. Doesn't anybody realize that? Same shit, different bucket. Don't ever forget that, boy. Because one day you're going to look back, like all kids, and hate me. You're going to blame me. It was my dad, you'll say. It's all his fault.'

'What's your fault?' I ask.

He looks at me, then takes a drink of whiskey from his coffee cup.

'Nothing,' he replies, setting the cup on the table. 'Absolutely nothing.'

For three days, I am sick. Neither Maggie nor Jonathan return. When I question Abderahim about them, he refuses to be truthful. Angry at his deception and simply tired of Tangier, I tell him I will be leaving.

'As you wish,' he says. 'One day you will return. I know.'

I look at him but say nothing.

I take the train to Marrakech, passing again through Casablanca and Rabat. I intend to stay in Marrakech, but upon arrival, I decide to take the bus to Essaouira, a small fishing port also known as Windy City, Afrika. Marrakech, I realize, is too busy, noisy, filled with color; I want *peace*.

'If you want peace,' a voice says, 'you would go home.'

I turn suddenly and look behind me. A veiled woman, draped entirely in black, looks at me. Do not look at me, her eyes say.

I turn away, looking at the clock above the ticket-teller's window. I have nearly two hours before the bus to Essaouira departs. In the meantime, I decide, I will sit and I will wait.

The bus station is hectic, filled with people, young and old, mostly old, and male: bearded men with brown, leathery skin and threadbare djellabas.

Though no longer sick, I am tired, sluggish; the heat flowing in through the opened doors is stifling. I undo the top three buttons of my short-sleeved shirt and gently fan the soft, cotton fabric against my belly.

A small, caramel-colored girl wearing faded, ill-fitting jeans and a pink Farrah Fawcett-Majors T-shirt stares at me. She is smiling, her huge, brown eyes wide with interest. I smile in return, and she raises her hand, curling her small, dirty fingers back and forth in a childish wave.

'Asalaam aleikum,' she says.

'Aleikum salaam,' I reply.

Putting her hands in her lap, she swings her bare feet back and forth and stares at me, still smiling. On either side of her are two elderly men, both bearded, sleeping, wearing white djellabas. Which, if either, of these men, I wonder, is the little girl's companion?

Upon departure, my relief to finally be leaving soon dissipates. There are at least fifteen more passengers than there are seats to accommodate them. Three people crowd into seats designed for two, with seven more men sitting cross-legged in the narrow aisle.

Several rows behind me, a young man holds a rusted parrot's cage filled with three fat chickens that cluck continually.

There is no air-conditioning.

By the time we arrive in Essaouira, I am as angry as I am frustrated. When the bus driver suggests that I pay him for passing me my bag from beneath the dilapidated bus, I push him aside and grab the bag myself. It is gray with dust.

'Go fuck yourself,' I snap, holding the bag to my side as I walk away.

'You,' I hear him yell, 'you don't tell me to fuck myself!'

I continue walking, expecting at any moment a stone or bottle to hit me in the back of the head. It does not come.

I rent a room for one week at the Hotel Riviera. Typical of most low-budget Moroccan hotels, it is clean and sparsely furnished, with stone-tiled floors and poorly lit hallways.

The room itself has two single-sized beds, a low, square nightstand between them, and a sink. The cracked, bluish-white walls are bare. Though the forty-watt bulb high above the sink offers little light, there are two huge windows that open onto the hotel's lower roof and, on either side, to other rooms.

There is no closet. I unpack, lying my clothes across one of the hard, narrow beds. It is early evening. Though I am not hungry, I decide to venture downstairs to the hotel's adjacent outdoor café—to eat a sandwich, perhaps.

As soon as I am seated at the café, I am approached by a young boy of seven or eight; holding a wooden box and a black rag, he offers me, in French, a shoeshine.

'Tomorrow,' I say. *'Damas. Oui?'*

'Oui, monsieur,' he replies, turning to the man at the table next to mine, offering the same.

The evening is cool but humid, and the café's tables are filled with Moroccan men, young and old; not a single female, of any age, is in sight.

The waiter, a tall, slender man in his early twenties, approaches and takes my order. He is pleasant, smiling, with the assured but humble manner typical of many Moroccan men his age.

Across from the café is a newsstand and telephone station. Next door is a tiny restaurant with a kitchen window and counter opened onto the street. Several teen boys loiter at its side, eating French fries from a greasy paper cone.

Further down the street, toward the edge of the huge plaza, known as the Place Prince Moulay Hassan, are several shops, selling, on either side, Moroccan art and rugs and the Thuja woodwork for which Essaouira is renowned.

My sandwich and espresso arrive. Thanking the waiter, I

begin to eat, to drink. I am, I realize, hungrier than I thought and I finish quickly and order another sandwich. While waiting, I sip the espresso and look at the people seated around me.

I think for a moment of Maggie but quickly push her from my mind; such thoughts frighten me.

I am approached by yet another young boy offering to shine my shoes. As with the earlier boy, I tell him to look for me tomorrow. This one persists, however, in English, setting his wooden box on the ground and saying:

'You can't let people see these shoes.'

I look down at my shoes.

'Look at them,' he says, pulling a rag from his back pocket. 'Just look at them.'

I look around. The previous boy is not in sight, so I tell the boy to go ahead, but to do so quickly.

When he is finished, I give him seven dirham; he thanks me, moving through the crowded tables in search of another customer.

'Maybe so,' I hear Jonathan say. 'But better that than some— some ugly American getting his shoes shined in the middle of the night by a seven-year-old kid.'

'A seven-year-old kid who needed the money,' Maggie replies. 'Don't forget that. Okay? Your little guilt trip probably cost that kid a meal.'

I close my eyes, absentmindedly scratching my forehead.

'Fuck it,' I whisper, slowly looking up.

I watch as a slim, middle-aged white woman wearing a huge, floppy hat and a light blue djellaba approaches the waiter, asking, in English, for bones.

Bones?

She is an unattractive women, pallid, with thin, sharp features and light brown hair, pulled back in a long, thin ponytail.

The waiter, behaving as if he knows her, tells her to wait, then walks into the café. He returns several minutes later with a white plastic bag that is filled, I imagine, with bones.

But what kind? I wonder.

The woman thanks him, putting the plastic bag in the large, straw purse she carries over her left shoulder. I watch with interest as she turns, head held high, and walks through the crowded tables past me. Who is she, I wonder, and what is she going to do with her bones?

'She's crazy,' I hear someone say.

I turn, looking at the man behind me. He smiles, holding up his large hand. On his middle finger, I notice, is a thick, silver ring.

'I was just wondering that,' I reply.

A black man, dark-skinned, he has thick, natty dreadlocks tied high above his head—like a fountain, I think—wrapped with a yellow, green, and black kerchief. He is wearing an orange, long-sleeved shirt, and around his thick neck, I am certain, is a snake-bone necklace.

'She lives here,' he says, 'just outside of town; she's been here since the seventies, apparently.'

His face is thick-featured, but angular, with eyes, I notice, like my father: huge, but narrow, almost Asiatic, and sloping. His skin is hairless, flawless, except for a thin, purplish keloid running diagonally across his right cheekbone.

'Without a scar he isn't even a man,' I hear my father say. 'He is merely male.'

'You know her?' I ask, turning sideways in my chair.

'Well,' he replies, smiling, 'anyone who's here for a while gets to know *of* her, anyway. Her name's Grace.'

His voice is deep, baritone on the verge of bass, with an indistinguishable accent—English, perhaps, or Jamaican? Eastern American? I cannot tell.

'What are those bones for?' I ask.

'She has a pack of dogs, apparently,' he replies. 'But—who knows?'

He leans back in his chair, laughing softly.

I look down the street and into the empty, lamp-lit plaza, then back at him.

'What's your name, brother?' he asks.

'Ulysses,' I reply.

'Good name,' he says. 'Strong name.'

He holds out his hand, pulling his fingers together into a fist, and says:

'I'm YaYa.'

I raise my hand, touching my fist to his, and reply:

'Hey there, YaYa.'

He nods his head, resting back in his chair, and takes a sip from his small glass of orange juice. Looking at me, he asks:

'Where you from, Ulysses?'

'Hollywood,' I reply.

'Hollywood? You an actor?'

'Well,' I reply, 'I'm not really from Hollywood; it's just a metaphor.'

He looks at me and laughs.

'So,' he says, 'you're a writer, then?'

He asks this as if he hopes it to be true.

'No,' I reply. 'I'm a dancer. I came to Morocco for, well, let's—let's just say here I am.'

'Here you are,' he says.

'And you?'

'Well, it's actually quite a coincidence,' he says, winking. 'Because—I'm from Hollywood, too.'

'Ah, okay,' I reply. 'A homeboy, then?'

'That's right,' he says, nodding his head, grinning.

'Are you a writer?' I ask.

'Funny you ask that,' he replies. 'Folks usually ask if I'm a musician.'

I raise my hand and point at the stack of papers on the table in front of him. He laughs.

'Well, yes,' he says. 'I guess this gives me away.'

I am tempted, briefly, to mention that my father was a writer or, rather, that he had written, and published, a book of poetry. I do not.

'Are you here to—?' I begin to ask.

'Am I here,' he interrupts, 'to write or to relax? Was that your question?'

'No,' I lie. 'I can see that you're writing. *What* you're writing, however, I can't see. Are you working on anything specific? That was my question.'

He is a quiet, for a moment, watching me. Then he says:

'I'm working on a history of American black artists overseas, mostly in Europe but here, too, in Africa.'

'Just artists?' I ask. 'Or writers and—'

'Writers are artists,' he says, again interrupting me. 'As are poets and musicians and—and dancers, too.'

'Are we now?' I reply.

There is a persistent, if subtle, condescension in his tone that I do not like; it reminds me, again, of my father.

'I think so,' he says. 'Whether you're a dancer or a writer or a singer, you're still taking what's inside and—and saying, *Hey, look at this. Look at what I've made.*'

'I guess so,' I reply, shrugging.

I no longer want to talk to him.

In the distance, I watch as one of the electric lamps surrounding the plaza flickers briefly and then with a faint pop burns out.

'How long you here for?' I hear him ask.

Still looking away, I reply:

'A week, at least, maybe longer; I don't know.'

'Well, I'm going to have to bend your ear before you leave; I'm warning you. I've been here for nearly a month and you're only the third brother I've seen.'

'I can believe it,' I say, looking at him.

'Though I'm concentrating on the more famous of—of our brethren,' he says, 'I'd be interested in getting your opinion of life overseas—as a man of color.'

'Life overseas,' I say. 'I see it's over.'

'Pardon me?'

'Sorry,' I reply. 'My grandfather used to say that; don't ask me what it means.'

He smiles.

I look at the thick twist and rise of his dreadlocks; the Lion of Zion, I think, remembering the name of a song or book.

'Jimi Hendrix spent a summer here, in Essaouira,' he says. 'That's why I'm here, actually; seems, though, he ate in every single restaurant and slept in every hotel—and everyone knew him personally.'

He shrugs.

'Like Elvis,' I reply, 'in Memphis. *Elvis ate here. Elvis slept here.*'

'Elvis ate fried peanut butter sandwiches and smoked reefer here,' he adds. 'Elvis died on the toilet here.'

He laughs; I smile.

'But because it's Elvis,' I hear a woman say, 'you think it's, God, almost Shakespearean. That's pathetic. Really, it is.'

I look at YaYa; he is looking at me.

'So,' I ask, 'you going to write about James Baldwin?'

'Of course,' he replies. 'I already have. I started with Josephine Baker, then the Harlem Renaissance artists, and worked up to Baldwin and—Angelou and Gordon Parks and Nina Simone.'

He speaks, I think, as if certain I am either omniscient or an idiot.

'I was in Paris before I came here,' he continues. 'Now I'm doing a bit of research on Hendrix—then back to Paris. I want to write a bit about Basquiat; see what I can find about him. I want to go to Ghana, too. And Kenya.'

'It must be fascinating research,' I say.

'It is,' he agrees, nodding his head. 'It's—it's a subject that's been written about before but only really as a footnote. What's most fascinating, and what the main theme of the book is, is that it was really black folk who created what we now know as the Bohemian sensibility—in every medium; painting, writing, music, philosophy. The *lifestyle.* It was a black thing.'

I watch him as he speaks, envisioning a drop of mercury as it rolls across his dark, smooth forehead, down the bridge of his nose, over his lips, down his chin, back up, and finally, into his mouth. His eyes slowly turn silver.

'Like rock and roll,' he continues, 'it was appropriated and popularized, mainstreamed, by white people, but Jack Kerouac, Ginsberg, Burroughs, all those guys, they stole everything they became famous for—from Zora Neale Hurston. Read her stuff, then theirs; you'll see.

I watch him and nod my head.

'There's not a single black writer considered a part—a major part, anyway—of the Beat movement,' he says. 'No. We get Kerouac writing about the sexy rhythm of the ghetto, but that's it. A footnote—and an offensive one, too. A cliché. I realized as much before I started my research, but that's what guided me, inspired me: the need to tell the truth.'

His tone softens, turning inward.

'Hell,' he continues, 'Billie Holiday was the icon, the mother, of modern bohemia, but now she's been transformed into—into some dead, black puppet mouthing parlor songs for fags and old white ladies on Central Park West.'

'Please,' I say, 'don't ever write my epitaph.'

'Billie gave birth to the Beat writers,' he says, ignoring my comment. 'Like Coltrane did, and Zora and Dizzy, even; they all did. Bessie and Langston and—'

He stops, abruptly, then says:

'Paris, modern-day Paris, even, wouldn't be what it is today, at least what it's considered to be, without black Americans. That's the truth, Ulysses.'

His use of my name surprises me.

'Malcolm X was banned for life from France,' I say. 'Did you know that?'

'I did,' he replies. 'I do—I mention it in my book. Because that's where the truly interesting spin comes in. French people are some of the most xenophobic, racist people on the face of the planet. They adore Josephine Baker in her banana skirt and James Baldwin writing about sex with white folk, but just try being a black man walking along the Champs Elysées at three in the morning. Then see what comes running.'

'I've tried it,' I say.

He smiles.

'Then you know of what I speak,' he says.

'I do.'

We talk for hours, until the café closes, then wander, still talking, through the Medina. It is, I think, as if I have never left Tangier; though obviously less populated, the Medina's streets and buildings are nearly identical: cramped, ancient, crumbling, with narrow, twisting, dead-end streets and darkened courtyards.

Since liquor is officially forbidden in the Medina, we leave, finding our way to a small, poorly lit bar near the beach. Other than an elderly Moroccan and two men arguing in Spanish, we are the bar's only patrons.

We order two Heinekens from the bartender and sit at a table near one of the windows; outside is the Atlantic Ocean, dark, endless.

As he hands us our Heinekens, the bartender tells us we have exactly one hour before the bar closes.

'Come back tomorrow,' he says, shuffling away.

'Was that an invitation?' YaYa asks. 'Or an order?'

'Neither,' I reply. 'It was a cry for help.'

We raise our bottles in toast, and each take a drink.

Later, before I fall to sleep, I lie with my eyes closed and think about YaYa. Do I like him? I wonder. He is witty and creative, intelligent, but he is also vain and condescending.

'Nobody hates a black man,' my father once said, 'like another black man. Even white folk won't say the nasty things a brother will say about another brother. And not just about another brother—about the whole black race.'

I think of my grandfather and his vicious diatribes, and I realize that my father was correct. Like women, I think, who are so much more critical of one another than men ever are.

'Nobody wants anybody to be free,' my grandfather once said. 'We're jealous of other people's freedom. We see someone who has what we don't—and we hate them. And it's not money or fame that causes the greatest jealousy; it's intelligence. It's happiness. It's *pride.* Nobody's more unloved than a proud man.'

I turn on my side, looking into the shadows. From the room next to mine, I hear a man coughing.

It's true, I think; though I like YaYa, like talking with him, it is his *pride,* his belief that he is correct, that I do not like. And I do not like it because I want to be the one who is correct; I want to be the *strongest.*

I close my eyes and soon fall asleep.

It is one of the rare times we have had guests. Seated around the kitchen table, with my father and grandfather, are three men I have not seen before. On the table, in front of each of them, is a cup of coffee.

'Nobody hates a black man,' my father says, 'like another black man. Even white folk won't say the nasty things a brother will say about another brother. And not just about another brother—about the whole black race.'

The men are silent, watching him.

'Now, what's *done* to a black man is a different story,' he continues. 'White folk still win the prize for out and out—'

He stops.

Though I am in the living room on the sofa, I can see and hear the gathering of men as they talk. My father turns, looking at me, and tells me to go outside. To my surprise, my grandfather insists that I stay.

'He needs to hear this,' he says, not looking at me.

'He's only eleven,' my father says, as if in explanation.

'Emmett Till was, what, fourteen?' one of the men asks, looking at me, then at my father.

'That he was,' my father replies, taking a sip of his coffee. He looks at me. 'Come in here, Ulysses,' he says.

I stand and walk into the kitchen.

Leaning against the side of the refrigerator, its surface cool against my bare back, I expect my father to speak to me; instead, the five men begin again to talk among themselves as if I am not even there.

I watch them, and I listen.

Though their story is one of terror, the men remain calm, emotionless, as they discuss the details. They sit quietly, listening, occasionally shaking their heads.

What I initially perceive to be their apathy frightens me; each of their faces is dark, still, empty. It is, I think, like looking into the blank, black eyes of a monster. Later, as a man, I will understand the nature of this silent rage, but now it leaves me speechless, unable to move.

'Used a staple gun,' one of the men says. 'Stapled it right to his chest. And left him there, like that, hanging from the telephone pole like some—'

Transfixed by their descriptions, it takes me a moment to realize that everyone is looking at me.

'Ulysses,' my father says, angrily, about to rise from his chair.

I look down, realizing with shame that I have wet myself. A puddle of urine between my bare feet, I look up at my father, my grandfather, at the men, and then run from the kitchen.

'Let him go,' I hear my grandfather say.

Out of the house, across the yard, and through the trees, I run, stopping finally at the river's edge. I look for a moment into the muddy, quick-flowing water, then close my eyes and jump.

Paddling to stay afloat, I look into the trees on either side of the river and try in vain to piss into the water. I imagine my father and grandfather, the three men, and I close my eyes, ashamed.

I swim to the riverbank, crawl from the water, and fall onto the grassy embankment. Turning over onto my back, I look up at the clouds that roll, as if pushed, across the dark, blue sky. A fly lands on my bare chest; I do not swat it away.

Behind me, in the trees, I hear a man whispering.

I sit straight, turning slowly to look into the shadowed forest behind me.

Hanging by his neck from one of the trees is a man. I do not recognize him. He is naked, light-skinned, with a hairy chest. Between his legs is a bloody hole; beneath the hole hangs a small, black mass. Stapled to his chest is piece of paper, red with blood. His hands are missing.

He opens his eyes, looking directly at me, and says:

'Emmett Till was only fourteen.'

I open my mouth, screaming. I do not stop until my father, kneeling at my side, grabs me by the shoulders, then hits me twice across the face.

'Ulysses!' he yells. 'Why are you screaming? What is wrong with—'

I pass out.

The next morning I am awakened by a knock at the door. It is YaYa, telling me to get out of bed. I look at the small, digital travel clock next to me; it is nearly noon.

'C'mon, dancerman,' he calls out. 'Get dancing.'

I look at the closed door, not moving, and tell him I will meet him downstairs, at the café, in a half hour.

'Make it fifteen minutes,' I hear him say. 'We have a lot to do today.'

I listen as his footsteps disappear down the hallway. One, I silently count, two, three, four, five, six, seven. I stop at twelve.

Throwing off the blanket, I sit up, stretching, and look at the clothes spread out on the bed across from me. I stand, walk to the sink, and brush my teeth. I wash my face and comb my hair, then pat it down. I get dressed.

For the next six, nearly seven, hours, I am questioned by YaYa about my life as a dancer, especially my time in Paris, Brussels, and Amsterdam. After lunch, we continue our conversation as we walk: through the Medina, along the beach, out into the nearby countryside.

'People think better when they walk,' he explains.

Much, but not all, of our conversation he tapes, using a small handheld recorder that he holds between us. He asks if the recorder bothers me; I tell him it does not.

Though I have told him of my previous two times in Essaouira, he stops frequently to point out particular sites of note. He takes me to the ruined pavilion buried in the sand near the beach and tells me that it was the inspiration for Jimi Hendrix's 'Castles in the Sand.'

'I know that,' I say.

'A lot of people don't,' he replies.

'And a lot of people do,' I remark.

He looks at me, as if in sudden recognition, and smiles; it's a response that I grow accustomed to as the day wears on.

As we walk through the high, stone walls of the Medina on our return to the hotel, he invites me to dinner.

'As payment,' he says, 'for letting me bore you.'

'I'd prefer money,' I reply.

He laughs heartily, slapping me roughly on the back.

It wasn't a joke, I think.

We agree to meet at eight o'clock in front of the hotel. Returning to my room, I stretch across the bed and close my eyes. Yawning, I kick off my shoes and turn sideways, resting my hands beneath the pillow.

I am startled awake soon thereafter by a sudden, loud knocking. Disoriented, I open my eyes and turn my head up toward the ceiling.

What time is it? I wonder.

I look at the clock on the table next to the bed; it is exactly eight o'clock.

I turn my head, looking at the door.

'Come in,' I say.

The door slowly opens; Maggie, wearing a dark red dress, stands in the doorway, smiling.

I sit up.

'Don't you know,' she says, 'no rest for the naughty?'

I look at her.

'Keep the lips,' she says, entering the room and shutting the door behind her.

She walks to the foot of the bed, puts her hands on her hips, and looks at me.

'What?' I ask.

She smiles.

'If you've eaten your tongue,' she says, 'don't eat your lips; you'll need them.'

I say nothing.

'Oh, forget it,' she says. 'I was just trying to be original. I was—I was going to ask if the cat got your tongue, but, well, it's been said before.'

She sits on the bed next to my feet and puts her hand on my leg. I pull away.

'Ulysses,' she says, 'what's—'

She becomes silent, watching me.

'Well,' she eventually continues, 'I'll wait for *you*, then.'

'Wait for *me?*'

She crosses her legs, resting her arms on her knees, and looks at me. She closes her eyes, gently biting her lower lip, then opens them and looks at me again.

'You have a lot of explaining to do, mister,' she says.

I shift my position, putting my feet on the floor.

'I have a lot of explaining to do?'

'Yes,' she replies, 'you do. But if you—'

'What the fuck happened to you?' I interrupt angrily. 'It wasn't very—'

I pause for a moment and finally ask:

'How did you find me?'

'Abderahim,' she answers, looking confused. 'He said you told him you were going to Essaouira.'

'No, I didn't,' I reply, standing and looking down at her. 'I told him I was going to Marrakech.'

I move away from the bed, next to the sink.

'In Marrakech,' I continue, 'I decided at the train station to take the bus here, to Essaouira. There's no way he could've known that.'

She looks at me and frowns.

'Ulysses,' she says, 'how would I know you'd be here if Abderahim didn't tell me? What is wrong with you?'

'What's wrong with me?' I reply. 'What's wrong with *you?*'

She is silent for a moment, leaning forward, her hands on the bed. She watches me suspiciously, then says calmly:

'You're scaring me, brother.'

I slowly shake my head in frustration.

'You disappear,' I say, 'playing some kind of crazy prank with Abderahim and then come here trying to—'

'Are you serious?' she asks, interrupting me. 'You can't be serious.'

We look at each other.

'Well,' I say. '*Something* happened. I don't know what it was or whose idea, but—something happened.'

She is silent for a moment, searching my face as if for a clue.

'Sweetie,' she says, 'for three days you were sick.'

Her voice is slow, monotonous.

'You couldn't even walk,' she continues. 'Whenever I could get away from Jonathan, I'd come to your room and sit, feed you, talk to you, whatever. I even bathed you. You don't remember that?'

I say nothing.

'Then on Thursday,' she continues, 'I came to see you, and you were gone—like that. I tried to ask Abderahim what had happened, but—you know him—all he would say is that you were going to Essaouira. So, here I am. Ulysses, you don't—*what* is wrong with you?'

She stares at me, pensive.

I put my hand on the edge of the sink and close my eyes.

'Ulysses?'

'I did not tell Abderahim I was coming here,' I say softly.

'Everything else you're saying is *possibly* true, but that isn't. And if you're lying about that, then you're lying about—about the rest, too.'

'Lying?' I hear her say. 'Why would I be lying?'

I open my eyes, watching her.

'You tell me,' I reply.

'My dear, confused boy,' she says.

She stands, walking around the edge of the bed toward me.

'You don't remember being sick?' she asks.

'I remember that.'

A foot away from me, she stops.

'You don't remember taking a shower in the wrong room?'

Watching her, I take my hand from the edge of the sink.

'I remember that, too,' I reply.

I become silent, my mind spinning, then continue:

'And I *remember* Abderahim telling me that there were no such—that you weren't even staying in the hotel; he had never seen you before.'

'If he said that,' she says, 'it was a joke. You know how irritable Abderahim is. But I didn't, I swear, have anything to do with it. Besides, how would I know any of this if I wasn't there?'

'Abderahim,' I reply. 'He could've told you. You could've planned to—'

'Ulysses,' she says, interrupting me, 'listen to what you're saying. Now imagine someone else is saying it.'

She steps forward, putting her hand on my shoulder, then comes even closer. She rises, kissing me on my neck. Looking up, she says:

'You were pretty delirious for those three days. Maybe you—maybe you got kind of confused. Do you think?'

I look at her mouth.

'I went to a party once in Houston,' she says, 'and woke up the next morning in New Orleans.'

'How did you find me here?' I ask, ignoring her comment. 'Here in this hotel?'

She steps back, looking at me, and replies:
'I asked.'
'Asked who?'
'Whoever. There's not exactly a lot of tall black American men walking around Essaouira, my brother. In case you haven't noticed.'

I think of YaYa.

'Ulysses?'

Though I am still convinced that Abderahim was unaware of my detour to Essaouira, I take a deep breath and shake my head in defeat.

How else, I wonder, could she have known?

'Fuck me,' I say softly.

'As you wish,' she replies.

I look out the opened window.

'That was a metaphor,' I say.

'It always is.'

'Where's Jonathan?' I ask, turning toward her.

'Tangier,' she replies, returning to the bed and sitting down. 'He wanted to come, but I told him I'd call when I found you. Now he hates you.'

'I'm sure he does,' I remark, shrugging.

She smiles.

'Well,' she says, 'he doesn't hate you, but he'd be content to never see you again. Or for me to never see you again. He seems to have forgotten that I've been irritated with him this entire trip, and he blames you for it. He wanted to know why I had to go look for you. He asked if I love you. Can you believe it? He's such a baby.'

I look at her.

'What we want,' I say, 'is someone to blame.'

She looks at me, confused for a moment, then says:

'Indeed.'

I look down at the floor, trying to make sense of the random thoughts and images shifting like a slideshow through my mind.

Again, I shake my head.

'Ulysses,' she says, 'come here and sit down.'

She pats the bed with her hand. I look first at her, then at the bed, then at the door.

'I don't want to think about this anymore,' I say, as if to myself.

'Then don't,' I hear her say.

I look at her and she smiles.

'I won't,' I say.

I walk to the end of the bed and bend over to put on my shoes. Standing straight again, I look at her and she returns my glance.

'You look beautiful in red,' I say.

'Well, you know,' she replies, 'same shit, different bucket.'

She takes a cigarette from her purse and lights it.

'So do you,' she says, slowly exhaling.

'So do I what?' I ask.

'Look beautiful in red.'

I peer down at my red shirt.

She takes a drag of her cigarette and smiles.

'I told you before,' she says, standing, 'I'm crazy, too. So don't worry about it. Just don't let it become a habit. Okay?'

She winks at me.

'Well,' I say, reaching for her hand, 'one of us is crazy; that's for certain. The question is: which one?'

In the farthest corner of the barn, behind two empty barrels, is a large cardboard box. Curious, I move the barrels aside and crouch next to it. Opening it, I find six dead pups wrapped in a wet, brown towel; their heads have been crushed.

Quickly replacing the towel and closing the box, I slide the barrels to their original position and stand, turning toward the barn door. I am crying.

'What are you doing?' my father asks.

I look up. He is standing in the doorway, silhouetted against the bright afternoon sunlight behind him.

'Nothing,' I reply. In an instant, I stop crying.

'Why are you crying?' he asks, remaining completely still. I cannot see his face.

'I'm not,' I reply, looking down at the barn's dirt floor.

'You're thirteen,' he says. 'You're too old to be crying.'

'I wasn't crying,' I say, still looking down.

'Yes,' he says, 'you were.'

I say nothing.

'We couldn't keep them,' he says. 'I had to kill them.'

'Why?' I ask, looking up at him.

'It doesn't matter why,' he replies. 'Now go on; do your chores.'

He turns, disappearing around the corner.

I find the hoe, leave the barn, and walk to the garden. Wondering where the dog is—whether she, too, has been killed—I look up and, far off in the pasture, see my grandfather walking slowly along the length of the barbed-wire fence.

What, I briefly wonder, is he doing?

As I slowly deepen the narrow, shallow ravine between the rows of corn, I stare down at the dry, loose dirt, lost in thought. From somewhere on the north side of the house, I hear the dog bark, and I am relieved.

I remember when my father, angry that I had forgotten to feed our previous dog, Pinky, took his rifle and shot her. Forcing me to watch, he shot her three times, then told me to bury her. Later that night, as I was getting ready for bed, he came into my room and apologized.

'When animals are domesticated,' he said, 'it is our responsibility to take care of them, to feed them. You have to learn that, Ulysses, and maybe now you have.'

I had wanted to say something, ask something, I wasn't sure exactly what.

'Yes, sir,' I replied.

I look out into the pasture again. My grandfather is still walking along the length of the fence. This time, however, he is walking in the opposite direction.

Is he searching for something? I wonder. If so, what?

My father has told me to deepen the ravines only slightly, to trap the rainwater without exposing the roots, but I slowly, purposefully, disobey him, digging deep into the bottom and side of each narrow ditch. He will give me a beating, I know, for disobeying him, but I do not, at the moment, care.

When I introduce Maggie to YaYa, I am struck momentarily by the suspicion that they know each other. As I watch them look at one another, then shake hands, I sense a mutual uneasiness or embarrassment. I am tempted to ask if they have met before, but I do not.

Around the corner from the hotel, we find a small, candle-lit restaurant specializing in Moroccan and French cuisine. Reminding me of a bordello or an opium den, its inner walls are draped with red velvet, and the large, softly padded armchairs are upholstered with black and gold brocade.

The restaurant is busy, noisy, and we are seated at the last remaining table, a corner banquette meant for six.

'If Mata Hari takes our order,' YaYa remarks, sitting down, 'I will not be surprised.'

Maggie, who is sitting next to me, across from YaYa, runs her hands across the smooth, shiny black tabletop.

'Is this stone?' she asks. 'It feels like it.'

YaYa leans sideways and looks beneath the table.

'I can't tell,' he replies, sitting straight, 'but I think so, yeah.'

'Fuck you both,' I say.

They both look at me.

'We've barely sat down,' I say, 'and already you two are casing the joint.'

They laugh.

Though it is forbidden to sell liquor within the walls of the

Medina, our waiter produces a wine list. We order a bottle of Merlot, a second with our meal, and a third when we are finished eating.

The waiter, a small, slender man with a pencil-thin mustache and slicked-back hair, looks at us, frowning.

'As you wish,' he says, taking the empty bottle and walking away.

'I don't think Pierre likes us,' Maggie says, lighting a cigarette.

'His name isn't Pierre,' YaYa says.

'Well,' Maggie replies, 'he looks like a Pierre, don't you think? Like a naughty Muslim who's changed his name to Pierre.'

I look at YaYa who is looking at Maggie. He smiles, I am certain, with desire. Suddenly, briefly, I hate him.

Our waiter returns and, in perfect imitation of a French waiter named Pierre, abruptly yet punctiliously pours our wine. When he is gone, we raise our glasses and offer a toast.

'To writers and dancers,' I say, 'and—'

I look at Maggie.

'Ladies of leisure,' she says, smiling as she takes a drag of her cigarette.

'To writers and dancers and ladies of leisure,' I agree.

'To books not yet finished,' YaYa adds.

'And dances not yet danced,' Maggie says, giggling.

We drink our wine, talking, laughing. They laugh; I smile.

The restaurant's other customers ignore us, as we ignore them, each party caught up in its own conversations and revelry. The restaurant becomes progressively louder and more raucous, filling with cigarette smoke, incense, and, from hidden speakers, a continual loop of ganoua music.

Twice, the candle on our table is replaced.

As we begin our fourth bottle of wine, we are approached by a short, plump woman with thick, wavy black hair parted on the side. Unusually pretty, with a light smattering of almond-colored freckles across her nose and cheeks, she is, I immediately assess, the daughter of a black woman and white man.

She is dressed in a tight, gold, short-sleeved sweater and skirt that accentuate her fleshy limbs and heavy belly, and I am reminded of my grandfather's words:

'Bones are for boys; meat is for men.'

The three of us look up at the woman. She smiles, her full, red lips parting to reveal perfect teeth.

What a beautiful smile, I think.

'Excuse me,' she says. 'I don't mean to bother you, but I was just over there with my friends—'

She turns her head, pointing across the crowded restaurant at a table of three frowning white women, each with matching blond haircuts that are short on the side, long on the top. They sit, stone-faced, and look at one another.

'Well,' she continues, looking back at us, 'I noticed you earlier and, well, I just wanted to come over and say hey. That's all. I'm from the States, too—California.'

Her voice is thin, girlish.

Maggie leans back in her chair, looking at the three white women across the restaurant, then sits straight and looks up at our visitor.

'Would you care to join us?' she asks, taking a drag of her cigarette.

As she says this, she puts her other hand on my thigh and squeezes it.

'Sure,' the woman replies, smiling. 'Let me just go check with my friends and—and see what they want to do. Okay?'

There is something familiar about her, something I can't quite fix.

'Of course,' Maggie says. 'Tell them to come over; we won't bite.'

'Unless you want us to,' YaYa adds.

The woman turns, looking at YaYa, and smiles.

'Well, then,' she replies, 'I'll definitely be back.' She returns to her table.

'My God,' Maggie whispers, turning toward me. 'What a *fat* ass!'

'Tell me about it,' YaYa replies, grinning, staring at the woman as she walks away.

'You're a pig,' Maggie says. 'I knew it when I met you.'

'You know what they say,' he replies. 'Bones are for boys; meat is for men.'

I look at him.

'My grandfather used to say that,' I remark.

'So did my father,' he replies. 'Smart men, I—'

'Hey,' Maggie interrupts. 'I'm sorry; I should've asked you two before I invited them over. Is that alright? She seems kind of—kind of strange. And those friends, my God!'

'No problem,' YaYa answers. 'The stranger the better. Besides, I think we've been rebuffed.'

He nods his head in the direction of their table. Maggie and I turn, looking. The three white women are walking out the door, looking at us and whispering, their eyes narrowed as they disappear into the night.

Their friend returns to our table, shrugging, with a glass of white wine in her hand. Her fingers, I notice, are short, chubby, the long fingernails painted a bright red.

'They were tired,' she says, 'but I'm not.'

YaYa slides across the banquette and pats it with his hand.

'Have a seat,' he says, looking at me and winking.

I take a drink of wine, looking at the woman as she sits next to YaYa, setting her purse between them. Wiggling her ass on the seat, as if to get comfortable, she looks up at the three of us, eyebrows raised, and smiles.

'What's your name, honey?' Maggie asks, leaning back in the chair and crossing her legs. With the hand that holds the cigarette, she reaches up and lightly strokes the back of her neck.

'Baby,' the woman replies.

Maggie looks at her, and asks:

'Baby?'

'Well, Gabriella,' she explains. 'But everyone calls me Baby.'

Maggie glances at me, then looks again at the woman.

'Well, Baby,' she says, 'I'm Maggie. This is Ulysses, and this is YaYa.'

'Hey, Baby,' I say.

'Pleased to meet you,' YaYa says, looking at her.

She looks at YaYa and smiles.

'Where are you guys from?' she asks, taking a drink of her wine.

'Hollywood,' YaYa says, looking at me. 'We're all from Hollywood.'

'That's right,' I say. 'Tinseltown.'

Maggie looks at me but says nothing.

'I used to live there,' Baby says. 'Well, in Glendale, but I worked in Hollywood. And I *don't* want to talk about it.'

Maggie looks at me, then at Baby.

'Okay,' she says, as if confused.

'It's too painful,' Baby explains.

'Okay,' Maggie repeats, shrugging.

Baby takes another drink of her wine, finishing it. I pick up the bottle immediately and raise it toward her. She nods her head, smiling, and accepts.

'Please,' she says. 'Thank you.'

I fill her glass, then set the bottle on the table.

'Where do you live now?' YaYa asks.

'San Fran,' she replies. 'I've been there for, oh, three, four years. Have you been?'

'I have,' he replies. 'Sorry, but I didn't like it.'

'Me neither,' I say.

'I hated it,' Maggie adds. 'Well, I didn't hate it, but I'd never go back; that's for sure.'

'That's okay,' Baby says, looking at each of us. 'I don't particularly like it either.'

It is obvious, though, that she does like it.

As the four of us talk and drink, it becomes increasingly apparent that Baby is either drunk or shameless—or a shameless drunk. Whatever she is, she is definitely a verbal exhibitionist.

Though warning us again and again that certain moments in her life are 'just too painful to discuss,' she proceeds to regale us relentlessly with the deeds and misdeeds of her nasty past.

'That reminds me of the time I was turning tricks in Montreal,' she says. 'Most of the other girls hated taking it up the ass, but, you know, I never—'

'You were a prostitute?' YaYa asks, interrupting her.

'Unfortunately, yes,' she replies. 'In Montreal, Cleveland, and, for a month, in Detroit.'

'Montreal? How did you—?'

'Well,' she says, 'I'd rather not talk about it. It's too painful to discuss.'

Slowly shaking her head, she takes a sip of her wine. YaYa and I watch her, waiting. Maggie yawns.

'Oh, Lord,' she continues, 'when I think of that time in my life, it's just so—oh, Lord. The hepatitis, the angel dust, the—the back-alley blowjobs and—'

'You have hepatitis?' Maggie asks, grimacing. 'A or B?'

'Well,' Baby replies, sadly, 'I'd rather not talk about it. It's too—'

'Painful,' Maggie interjects, pinching my leg beneath the table. Baby nods her head.

She proceeds to tell us of her various abusive boyfriends, her life as a topless waitress in Las Vegas, the addiction to heroin, mescaline, acid, and alcohol, and her seven years of therapy.

'But I wouldn't be who I am today,' she explains, 'if I hadn't walked through the fire, you know? It's like—'

Looking first at her watch, then around the empty restaurant, Maggie interrupts Baby to suggest that we leave.

'You have had such a fascinating life,' she says, smiling sympathetically at Baby, 'and I'd love to hear more about it. *But* it's getting late, sweetie, and I want to go for a walk before I go to bed. Okay?'

Baby excuses herself to use the washroom, taking her purse, and totters drunkenly away from the table. Maggie watches her and then turns toward us, frowning.

'Too painful to discuss,' she says. 'Please.'

YaYa laughs.

'Gang-banged by seven of the Harlem Globetrotters!' Maggie exclaims, placing her hands beneath her breasts and leaning forward. 'Can you believe that ho? But ask her if she has hepatitis A or B, and suddenly it's too painful to talk about.'

YaYa doubles over in his seat, laughing; he is drunk.

'Skanky bitch,' Maggie continues. 'Wearing that over-used snatch of hers like a badge of honor!'

'Damn, girl,' I say, placing my hand on the back of her warm neck. 'Don't hold anything back.'

She looks at me, smiling, and winks, reaching up and putting her hand on mine.

'I'm just playing,' she says. 'But, really, that bitch is too much. Like we needed to know the color of the *cotton* panties she was wearing when that encyclopedia salesman molested her. Please.'

I feel a drop of urine soak into my underwear. I shift in my seat.

'Well,' YaYa says, trying to stop laughing, 'now we have something to talk about.'

'And how now, brown cow,' Maggie replies, giggling.

She takes my hand from the back of her neck, places it on her leg, and then says:

'I bet half of that shit isn't even true. She's probably on the toilet right now playing with herself, thinking about it.'

YaYa again doubles over, laughing.

'Oh, God,' Maggie says, giggling. 'I'm awful, just awful.'

She leans sideways and puts her head on my shoulder.

'Yes,' I say, 'you are.'

Baby returns and, after paying, we leave.

Outside, Maggie suggests we walk to the Medina's ramparts. Though Baby informs us that access is forbidden at such a late hour, we decide to go anyway.

'Who knows?' Baby says cheerily. 'Maybe I'm wrong.'

Though the entryway leading to the ramparts is, in fact, closed, it is not locked. Maggie and I push the high, iron gate open; slipping through, we run silently up the walkway to the stone parapet. Baby and YaYa are behind us, walking slowly. They hold hands, whispering.

Standing next to one of the huge, rusted cannons, I put my arm around Maggie's waist and look out across the darkened ocean. Far below us, huge waves crash across the rocky shoreline, rolling up against the mammoth stone walls of the rampart, then pulling back into the violent swirl and tide of the ocean. A fine, cool mist rises, as if falling, and then settles lightly upon our bare flesh. Shivering, Maggie moves closer, hugging me. I kiss the top of her head, holding her, and stare into the night.

'I'm drunk,' she whispers.

'Yes, you are,' I say.

'But still pretty,' she replies, giggling.

Somewhere behind us, in the shadows, I hear YaYa laughing.

'Kitten!' I hear Baby yell.

Maggie squeezes me tighter, gently rubbing the side of her face against my chest.

'I'm glad I found you,' she says.

Looking up at me, she smiles.

'Oh, God,' she says, groaning. 'That sounded corny, didn't it? Sorry.'

I rub my hands across her back but say nothing.

'Watch this,' she says, suddenly pulling away from me.

She turns, taking the translucent, white scarf from her shoulders, holding it high above her head, and then lets it flutter, like smoke from a cigarette, in the cool ocean breeze.

'Don't let it go,' I say.

'Why not?' she asks, letting it go.

Hanging in midair, the scarf begins to fall, then rises, suddenly, fluttering as if alive, and then drifts, slowly, into the darkness, visible, then invisible; finally, it disappears.

His hands on the steering wheel, my father stares ahead at the road before us. Occasionally, I turn, glancing at him, but I, too, remain silent, staring out the opened window at the lush, green countryside.

Somewhere out there, I think, is an elephant.

Earlier this morning, surprising me, my father asked if I wanted to see a movie. After a moment, I replied:

'Sure.'

For the rest of the morning and afternoon, I am anxious, even nervous. At fourteen, I have never been to a movie. In fact, I have never been anywhere with my father not related to duty, to work. Why, I am curious, has he now invited me to both a movie and dinner?

The possibilities are endless.

In the pickup, as we near the city limits, I remember my grandfather as he stood in the doorway to my bedroom, watching me change, get ready.

'Paying good money,' he says, 'to watch rich, white folk pretend to be poor. How pathetic. How sad.'

'I've never been to a movie, Grandpa,' I reply, sitting on the bed and putting on a clean pair of socks, 'but I think there's black folk in them, too.'

My tone is vaguely sarcastic.

'There sure is,' he replies, 'and they're either the first to die or the first to kill.'

I remain silent, hoping he'll go downstairs and leave me alone. Soon, grumbling, he does.

In the theater, my father and I sit side by side, near the aisle. There are approximately twenty other patrons besides ourselves. I am surprised that more than half of them are also black. Why I am surprised by this, I do not know. I am thrilled as I sit there, looking around, eating the licorice sticks my father has taken from his jacket pocket.

'They charge an arm and a leg here,' he says, passing me the soft paper bag of candy, 'for the same thing.'

When the movie starts, I am suddenly disappointed. It is an old movie, filmed in black-and-white, with actors I have never heard of. I turn, looking up at my father, who is sitting, his hands splayed on his thighs, and staring intently at the screen.

Resigned, I soon settle into my seat, sucking on a piece of licorice, and watch the movie.

At least I'm here, I think.

The name of the movie is *Stormy Weather*. Nearing its end, I am pulled from my resignation by the appearance of the Nicholas brothers, two black men in tuxedos who move as I have never imagined possible.

I sit, as if hypnotized, and watch the two brothers fill the screen, side to side, top to bottom, with a force that I am simply unable to define. I am stunned.

After the credits have rolled and the theater's lights have risen, I realize, looking up at my father, that the movie has ended. He stands in the aisle, next to his seat, and smiles at me; it is a smile I will never forget.

'You liked it, huh?' he says.

I nod my head, slightly dazed. He stands, not moving, and looks at me. He seems to understand. Abruptly, he turns, looking up the aisle toward the exit, then back at me.

'Well, son,' he says, 'come on, let's go.'

I stand and walk past him. As I do, he puts his hand on my shoulder. Though I barely feel it, I will remember it later.

Leaving the theater, we walk across the street and eat dinner at a small Chinese restaurant. We eat in silence at first. Finally, I look up and ask my father if he has seen the dancing brothers before.

'In a movie,' I quickly add.

He sets down his fork and, tilting his head sideways, looks over my left shoulder.

'When I was a boy,' he replies, as if lost in thought, 'younger even than you, Dad used to take me to a movie nearly every weekend.'

'Really?' I ask.

'Yes, sir,' he answers. 'Back then there was a theater just for—

well, they called us *colored* back then, and we had our own theater. And out of all the movies I saw there, the one we saw tonight was my favorite. I saw it three times.'

I watch my father as he resumes eating and then look down at my plate. It is difficult, I think, to imagine my father and grandfather sitting in a theater, side by side, watching a movie. It is even more difficult to imagine them enjoying it. Especially my grandfather.

Bravely, I look up from my plate.

'Dad,' I say.

'Yes,' he replies, looking at me.

'Did you ever—did you ever dance?'

'Well,' he says, after a moment's thought, 'not like the Nicholas brothers; that's for certain.'

'What about—'

'Ulysses,' he interrupts, 'just get eating; we have a long drive ahead of us.'

I look down at my plate, suddenly embarrassed.

'Yes, sir,' I say, picking up my fork.

Later, as we walk to the truck, my father stops in front of a small second-hand bookstore and looks at the books in the window. Surprising me again, he suggests we go inside.

'But just for a moment,' he says.

Inside, I rush through the aisles, searching for the film section. Hoping to find something, anything, about the Nicholas brothers, I am soon disappointed.

Eleven different books about Marilyn Monroe, I grimace, but not one about them.

The clerk, an elderly white man with thick, silver hair, is watching me; I ask if he has heard of the Nicholas brothers.

'No,' he says.

I stand between the two bookshelves and look at him.

'They're dancers,' I explain.

He takes a deep breath and points his long, thin finger at the floor by my feet.

'On the bottom shelf,' he explains, 'is a small dance section.'

'Thank you,' I say, kneeling and leaning sideways as I scan the row of twenty, maybe thirty books. I find a book, *Black Dance in America*. Taking it from the shelf, I stand and smile, flipping open to the index. There, under N, I read, *'Nicholas Brothers, Harold, Fayard, pp. 201–211.'*

'Ten pages,' I whisper, shutting the book and rushing to look for my father. Finding him, I hold up the book and say:

'Please.'

He looks at the book's cover and frowns.

'How much is it?' he asks.

'Two dollars,' I reply.

He nods his head.

At home in bed, I switch on the lamp and open the book. After looking first at the three pictures of the Nicholas brothers, I then turn to the ten pages about them; I read the section twice.

The book on my lap, I look up at the darkened ceiling, thinking.

'You better get to sleep, boy,' I hear my father call out.

'Yes, sir,' I reply, looking at the opened door.

I close the book, setting it on the floor beside my bed, and turn off the lamp. Settling into the bed, I pull the blankets up to my chest and close my eyes. Soon, I am asleep, dreaming. I am free.

Showering, I listen to YaYa, in the stall next to mine, tell me of his night with Baby. Though I cannot see him, I can imagine the wide grin on his face as he talks.

'She was a freak,' I hear him say, 'a stone-cold freak. You know, I'm not one to talk about, you know, what happens behind closed doors, but, Lordy, was she a freak. Lordy, Lordy.'

'I could've told you that,' I reply, vigorously lathering soap beneath my arms. 'So could've Maggie.'

He laughs.

Lowering my head, I step beneath the rush of water, watching as the soapsuds swirl down the drain beneath my feet. In the corner of the shower, I suddenly notice, is a small, lime-green frog. It sits motionless for a moment, then slowly hops away, disappearing beneath the wooden door.

I finish showering quickly, turn off the water, and dry myself. Wrapping the damp towel around my waist, I step out of the shower stall. The frog is gone.

'You going to get something to eat?' YaYa asks, looking at me from above the blue wooden door of his shower.

'Yeah,' I reply, looking at him. 'Maggie's downstairs already. Come down when you're done.'

'Will do,' he says, tilting his head beneath the steaming water and rinsing the soapsuds from his dreadlocks.

It is a hot, sunny afternoon. Maggie and I sit at the outdoor café, drinking orange juice and peppermint tea.

Surprising me, Maggie is wearing neither a long skirt, nor scarf; she is wearing, instead, a yellow T-shirt with the single word, *'Moshood,'* emblazoned in red across her bosom. Above her hair, tied in a knot at the nape of her neck, she wears a red kerchief. Two huge, gold-hoop earrings, the sort popular in the seventies, dangle from her ears.

'New look,' I say. 'It's nice. You look pretty.'

'Pretty?'

'Yes,' I reply, smiling, 'pretty. What were you hoping for? Foxy?'

'Well,' she says, folding her slender arms, 'I was actually hoping for beautiful—but pretty will do.'

'I was going to say beautiful,' I reply, 'but I was under the impression you hated such compliments.'

'Compliments for the sake of compliments,' she explains, exasperated. 'Not truthful ones.'

She winks at me.

'Well, then,' I reply, 'you look beautiful.'

'Too late,' she giggles.

YaYa soon joins us, carrying several folders, a thesaurus, and a stack of papers. Setting it all on the table in front of him, he orders two glasses of orange juice and apologizes for having to write while we visit.

'Some of us have to work for a living,' he says, flipping through the stack of papers as if in search of something.

'Old man river, huh?' Maggie asks, winking again at me.

'Lift that bale,' I continue the joke. 'Tote that barge.'

'House niggas,' YaYa says, looking up at us, smirking. 'Lazy-ass house niggas.'

'Kittens!' a woman suddenly screams.

The three of us turn in unison to see Baby rushing toward us through the crowded tables. She is dressed in a manner nearly identical to Maggie's normal attire: a long red skirt, a black tank-top, an orange scarf wrapped across her shoulders and over her arms.

Maggie turns toward YaYa and says:

'Kittens?'

He shrugs and smiles.

Acting suddenly apathetic, Baby informs us that her three companions departed for Ourzazate earlier this morning. One of them, she says, is her girlfriend of seven months.

'You're a lesbian?' Maggie asks.

'No,' Baby replies, shrugging, 'I'm bisexual.'

'And your girlfriend?'

'Well, she's a lesbian. They all are. That's why they left. They were upset that I never came back to the hotel last night.'

She looks at YaYa, smiling.

'What bothered them most?' Maggie asks, taking a drag of her cigarette. 'That you cheated on your girlfriend? Or that it was with a man?'

'Who cares,' Baby answers. 'Hey, can I have one of your cigarettes? I haven't had a chance to buy any yet.'

Maggie reaches for the cigarette pack; with her thumb and middle finger, she flicks it across the table's surface toward Baby.

'Help yourself,' she says.

'Thanks, kitten,' Baby replies, picking up the cigarettes.

'Baby,' Maggie says.

'Yes,' she responds, holding one of the cigarettes between her plump fingers.

Her fingernails, I notice, are no longer red; they are purple.
'Please don't call me kitten,' Maggie says. 'I don't like it.'
Baby looks up at her.
'Unlike him,' Maggie adds, smiling at YaYa, who raises his right eyebrow as if to say, *What?*
'I didn't mean to offend you,' Baby remarks, lighting her cigarette and taking a drag.
'You didn't offend me,' Maggie explains. 'You irritated me.'
YaYa and I look at each other.
'Well, *Maggie,*' Baby replies, 'it won't happen again.'
'Thank you,' Maggie says, flicking the ash from her cigarette onto the ground.
Later, leaving Baby and YaYa at the café, Maggie and I wander out of the Medina. Walking along the beach, we watch a group of teenaged boys playing soccer. As we pass, a ball skids alongside us out into the water. Maggie turns and runs after it.
A perfect ass, I think, watching her.
Grabbing the ball, Maggie skips out of the water and onto dry land, and then kicks it back to the group of boys, who stand, as if in awe, watching her.
'Thank you!' a boy hollers.
'De rien,' Maggie replies, waving.
'Come on,' another boy hollers as we turn to leave. 'Come play.'
Maggie looks up at me and asks:
'Do you want to?'
'Sure,' I reply.
We turn and jog over to the group of boys. Maggie kicks off her sandals and rolls up the hem of her jeans. She takes off her earrings and slips them in her back pocket.
The boys watch her, smiling.
'Watch out, watch out,' one of them says with a laugh; the other boys cheer, also laughing.
'That's right, men,' Maggie replies. 'You better watch out.'
Winking at me, she delicately smoothes her hair, pinkies raised, and then, surprising everyone, rushes suddenly at the ball

and begins to kick it, unimpeded, across the beach toward two logs that are, I presume, a makeshift net.

The boys erupt into cheering and laughing, half of them chasing after her.

By the time we leave, Maggie has made three goals and fourteen new friends. She waves, promising to return tomorrow, and we again wander off along the beach. The boys call out behind us, laughing and talking in Arabic, and soon resume their game.

'I feel like Jack Kennedy,' I say, holding her hand, 'when he said he would be forever known as the man who accompanied Jackie to Paris.'

'Jackie Onassis,' she scoffs. 'Please. That cunt.'

She laughs.

Silently, we walk past Hendrix's castle in the sand and, moving inland, toward the rolling dunes that stretch further in the distance to the low, shrub-covered hills. Soon, we are unable to see either the beach or Essaouira's crumbling, white skyline. Around us, there is only sand; above us, only sky.

Releasing my hand, Maggie steps away from me, then down the steep, soft incline of a sand dune. Midway, she stumbles and falls forward, rolling sideways to the curving basin between the rising hills of fine, brown sand.

She sits straight, laughing, and looks up at me.

'Come down here,' she says.

At her side, still standing, I watch as she pulls the kerchief from her hair, then raises her arms and takes off her T-shirt. She is not wearing a brassiere.

She stands and takes off her jeans and white panties. She begins to walk away, but then abruptly stops and turns toward me.

I stand where I am and look at her: from her face to her neck to the chestnut-brown circles of her nipples, down her smooth belly to her belly button to the triangle of trimmed, black hair between her legs. I look at her legs, the insides of her thighs, along the length of her calves to her ankles, and finally to her sand-flecked feet.

I begin to undress. First, I drop my pants in the sand, then take off my shirt. She stares at my crotch, smiling. I take off my underwear, then hang them on my erection.

Maggie laughs, then says:

'Pig.'

My hands at my side, I jiggle my cock, causing the underwear to fall.

Again she laughs.

'You boys are so talented,' she says.

I look down at my cock and continue, with my hands at my side, to jiggle it up and down, side to side.

'Okay, you can stop now,' she says, frowning. 'It's starting to give me the creeps.'

I stop and look up at her. We smile at each other but do not move. We stand, perhaps fifteen feet apart, and simply look at one another's nakedness in the bright, hot afternoon sun.

As I watch, she moves her right hand across her belly and down between her legs. Staring at me, she begins to stroke herself, gentling parting her labia and then slowly inserting her index finger into the soft, pink folds.

'Have you ever wondered,' she asks, her hand still moving gently between her legs, 'why I never ask you about your father?'

Pulled from my thoughts, I look up at her face; her eyes are now closed.

'What?' I ask.

'I mean,' she says softly, 'here you are, someone I've only just recently met. You tell me that you've killed your father, though you later deny it, kind of, and other than that one time in Tangier, I never bring it up. Don't you wonder why?'

'No,' I reply, looking between her legs, then again to her face, 'I don't.'

'Maybe you should,' she says, opening her eyes.

'Maybe I will,' I reply, stepping toward her.

'Stop,' she demands. 'Just watch me.'

I stop, taking hold of my erection, and begin to slowly stroke it.

'You're the boss,' I say.

'Did you do it?' she asks, slowly moving her finger in and out of her vagina.

I take a deep breath and slowly exhale.

'Do what?' I ask.

'Kill your father,' she replies.

'You've asked me that before,' I say.

'I'm asking you again. Now.'

'No,' I reply, 'I didn't.'

'Are you positive?'

'Yes.'

'Are you sure?'

'No.'

I continue to stroke my cock and stare between her legs.

'You're not sure?' she asks.

'Yes.'

'What?'

'No.'

She is silent for a moment, raising her free hand and stroking the shadowed curve between her breasts.

'How did you do it?' she asks.

'Let me fuck you, baby,' I reply. My mouth is dry.

'Tell me how you did it,' she persists.

I am silent, staring at her as I stroke myself.

'You're crazy,' I say.

She lowers both her hands and steps slowly across the warm sand toward me. I look up at her face. She places both her hands on my chest and kisses me below the neck. I shudder, raising my hands, and pull her close against my body.

'So are you,' she whispers.

Gently, I lower her onto the warm sand and kneel between her legs. She looks up at me, silent, emotionless. Leaning forward, I take my cock and rub its swollen head between the warm, moist folds of her pussy.

Arching her back, she turns her face away from me, softly

moaning. Slowly, I put my cock inside of her. I lower my head and kiss the side of her neck, then whisper in her ear:

'I strangled him.'

'New York, huh?' he says. 'Ulysses, do you know how many young people have gone to New York with the hope of becoming a star?'

'I didn't say I wanted to be a star,' I reply. 'I said I wanted to be a dancer. I want to dance.'

He is silent, looking at me.

'Sit down,' he says, tapping the kitchen table with his knuckles.

I sit down across from him and fold my arms. He says nothing, looking at the floor. Turning toward me, he puts both his hands on the table and says:

'You can be sure I won't try to stop you from finding out for yourself,' he says. 'I knew you'd leave; knew it before even you did. But I'll warn you right now, boy: you'll be back.'

'To visit,' I reply, hating him.

'To visit,' he repeats, 'and eventually to live. You'll be back to live.'

'No,' I reply, 'I won't. I'll die before I come back here to live.'

He looks at me as if lost in thought.

'I hope you're right,' he says, surprising me.

'I know I'm right,' I reply.

'My father was a quiet man with a vicious temper,' I say, passing Maggie a joint. 'And he was far from loving. But I sure didn't want to kill him. I mean, there wasn't enough anger there for me to want to kill him. He was just another man I didn't get along with. That's all.'

She takes the joint, holding it to her lips.

'Granted,' I say, 'he got meaner as the years went by. Well, it's funny, because he got less mean with me, less violent, but he got crankier, in general, bitterer—bitter, he got more bitter.'

Maggie looks at me, puffing several times on the joint, inhaling deeply, then returning it.

'Now, my grandfather, I could've killed,' I continue, taking the joint and holding it. 'Him, I could've strangled to death with my bare hands. He was a—'

Suddenly I stop, looking down at the floor. It's as if I've forgotten something. The thought vanishes just as abruptly, however, and I look up again at Maggie.

'He was,' I continue, 'a vicious, bitter, smart, violent man—right to the end. And I could easily have killed him. Hell, I wish I had. But I didn't. And I didn't kill my father.'

I puff on the joint, holding the smoke in my lungs, and look at her.

'Liar,' she says, leaning against the headboard and clasping her hands behind her head.

I shake my head in frustration, exhaling.

'I think you *want* me to have killed him,' I say. 'Is that what you want? I've heard—read—that there's a certain kind of woman who gets turned on by murderers.'

I take another puff, watching her.

'Obviously, you don't owe me anything,' she says, leaning forward and holding out her hand, 'but what I would *like,* if nothing else, is the truth. I'm—I'm tired of these silly games.'

'Silly games?' I exclaim. 'How the hell am I playing silly games?'

I pass her the joint, then lean my shoulder against the door and fold my arms, looking at her.

Though the light above the sink is turned off, the room is softly lit with the dim, late-afternoon sunlight coming through the huge, opened windows.

'Either you killed your father,' she says between puffs, 'or you didn't. You told me the night we met that you did. The next afternoon, in the café, you told me that you didn't, but then you said that you might've. Earlier today, you said you did; now you say you didn't. *Those* are the games I'm talking about.'

Maybe, I think to myself, I just don't care.

'Now, it's bad enough that you say one thing one day and another thing the next,' she continues. 'But saying you've killed your father isn't quite the same as what most people will lie to strangers about, you know. Like you're a blackbelt in Karate, or—or that your mama's rich and your daddy's good-looking. I mean, if you had said that all this talk of killing your father was some type of metaphor, well, I could understand. But you didn't say that; you said you strangled him. That's pretty specific. And then—and *then* this whole business of disappearing from Tangier and saying you thought it was me who had disappeared.'

'I told you what happened with that,' I reply, realizing, suddenly, that I had forgotten about it.

'Yes, you did,' she says. 'And on its own it's not such a big deal. I mean, who hasn't freaked out or—or blacked out, or whatever. But when added to a confession of murder and—oh, let's not forget the fact that you did admit to blacking out in the past and—'

'I didn't say I blacked out,' I interrupt. 'I said I sometimes forget what I've done. There's a difference. I get preoccupied; that's all.'

She leans forward, laughing. Smoke drifts from her opened mouth.

'What the fuck do you think blacking out is?' she asks. 'It's forgetting what you've done.'

I look down at the floor, then close my eyes.

'Well?' I hear her say.

I look up.

'Well what?' I ask.

She groans, as if exasperated, then snuffs out the joint in the ashtray on the nightstand.

'Are you blacking out now?' she asks, sarcastically.

'Zoning out,' I reply. 'Not blacking out.'

'Oh, I see,' she says, giggling. 'You're stoned, I take it.'

'Boned?'

'I said *stoned*, you idiot.'

'Just keeping you on your toes,' I reply, winking.

'Whatever. Now answer my question, damnit.'

'I don't know,' I say softly.

'Know what?' she asks.

I say nothing.

'Know what?' she repeats loudly, sounding angry.

'I don't know whether or not I—whether or not I killed my father. I don't remember. I don't think I did. I don't have any memories of doing it. But I don't have *any* memories of that day, period, other than when I buried him. Well, I do remember a spot of blood on his face, but I don't know where it came from.'

'Maybe you shot him,' she says.

'I would've remembered that,' I reply.

She is silent, watching me closely.

'I have a wonderful way of compartmentalizing things,' I say, grinning.

'Like all men,' she replies.

'If I don't want to think about something,' I continue, 'I don't. I tell myself to stop—and I stop. Like that. It's not that I forget about it, not really. I just put it away in—in a compartment.'

'And you think that's what you've done with what happened?'

'No. Well, I don't think so. Like I said, I don't necessarily forget about the things that have happened. It's like—like the sky: Unless it's storming, I'm aware that it's there, but I don't think about it. I don't question it. You know?'

'Let me ask you this: Why do you think you *might* have killed him?'

'Because I don't remember *not* killing him,' I reply, laughing, 'and I keep having these strange thoughts and dreams and—I don't know.'

'And all this is funny to you?' she asks, frowning.

'There's different kinds of laughter, Maggie,' I reply, as I stop laughing, 'and very few of them are a result of something funny.'

'How philosophical of you,' she says, smirking. 'You should wear a beret.'

I give her the finger.

'Hey!' she suddenly exclaims, ignoring me. 'Was your father sick? Maybe it was a mercy killing.'

'No,' I reply, shaking my head, 'he wasn't sick. Well, he had been acting strange, kind of like he had Alzheimer's, but more ornery than anything. Not anything that would warrant a—a mercy killing.'

Her shoulders slump, as if in defeat, and she clucks her tongue.

'Maggie,' I say.

'What?' she replies, looking up at me.

'Let me ask *you* a question.'

'Go ahead.'

'Well, it's more of an observation than—than a question.'

'So?'

'Well,' I begin. I speak slowly, deliberately, as if reading from a menu. 'You don't seem bothered by any of this. I mean, you're curious, it seems, but not, you know, bothered.'

'And?'

'And doesn't it seem like most people would be bothered, somehow, by a man they've just met confessing to—to killing his father? Unless, of course, you are one of those women who—'

'A bank-robber might turn me on,' she says, interrupting me, 'but not a murderer, for God's sake. Well, a murderer could probably turn me on, but not *because* he's a murderer.'

'That doesn't answer my question.'

'You said it was an observation, not a question.'

I shrug and close my eyes, shaking my head.

'You can stop now,' I hear her say.

I open my eyes.

'What?'

'You can stop shaking your head and pass me my purse.'

I lean forward, picking her small, red-sequined purse off the floor, and pass it to her. She takes it, opens it, and begins rummaging through the jumbled contents. Unable to find what she is looking for, she turns the purse upside down and spills its contents onto the bed.

'Here we go,' she says. 'Watch this.'

She picks up a safety pin, bends, then straightens it, and looks at me.

'Open your eyes,' she demands.

'They are open,' I reply.

'Oh, God,' she says, groaning. 'You're pathetic. Really, you are.'

I shrug.

She looks at me and frowns.

'Anyway,' she says, rolling her eyes, 'just stay with me, okay?'

Again, I shrug.

'*Okay?*'

'Okay,' I reply.

I watch as she raises the safety pin and, opening her mouth as if to show me what is in inside, pushes its tip through her cheek. Raising her left hand, she puts her index finger inside her mouth and, with her thumb, snaps the safety pin shut.

'See?' she says, the pin's rounded end hanging over her bottom lip. 'No blood. No pain.'

I say nothing but continue to watch her; I am beginning to get an erection.

She unsnaps the safety pin, then pulls it like a sliver out of her cheek. Gently tapping the smooth, unblemished skin with her middle finger, she then tosses the pin onto the bed and smiles at me.

'You should see how people react,' she says, 'when I do it in a bar.'

I lower my hand, squeezing my erection through my trousers.

'This turns you on?' she asks, raising her eyebrows.

'You turn me on,' I reply.

'I'm sure I do,' she says, beginning to pick up her belongings from the bed and return them to her purse. Once done, she retrieves a small, silver tube, unscrews its lid, and applies a thick layer of dark red lipstick. Finished, she drops the tube into her purse, then sets it next to the bed.

'Does this turn you on?' she giggles.

'Its possibilities do,' I reply, unbuttoning my trousers.

I step back unsteadily, resting against the wall, and slowly undo my zipper.

'Did your father have a big dick?' she asks.

'No,' I reply. 'But my son does.'

'Your son?'

'Yeah,' I reply, 'my son. Ulysses.'

She looks at me and smiles, then leans forward and slowly crawls, on her hands and knees, to the end of the bed.

'Tell me all about him,' she whispers.

'And Noah began *to be* a husbandman, and he planted a vineyard. And he drank of the wine, and was drunken. And he was uncovered within his tent. And Ham, the father of Canaan, saw the nakedness of his father and told his two brethren without.'

I look up at the wall, thinking, then return to the opened book before me.

'And Shem and Japheth took a garment, and laid *it* upon both their shoulders, and went backward and covered the nakedness of their father. And their faces *were* backward, and they saw not their father's nakedness.'

And how, I wonder, did they do that?

'And Noah awoke from his wine,' I continue, 'and knew what his younger son had done unto him. And he said, Cursed be Canaan; a servant of servants shall he be unto his brethren.'

I set the Bible on the desk.

'A servant of servants shall he be unto his brethren,' I repeat, looking out the bedroom window.

Why, I wonder, would Canaan, rather than his father, Ham, be cursed? Why, indeed, would either one of them, in such a circumstance, be cursed?

It is not, I think, as if a laughing Ham had invited the neighbors to look at his father, naked and drunk, in the tent. No. He told his brothers, and then they covered their father.

What, then, I wonder, did Ham initially tell his brothers? *If you want a good laugh, boys, go check out Dad; he's naked in his tent.* Or, perhaps, *Hey, Dad's passed out naked; let's shave his entire body and paint him blue.*

The thought of it makes me smile.

The passage, I think, is like so much of the Bible, confusing not for what it says but for what it doesn't say.

The basic premise, it would seem, is that it is sinful to see one's father naked. But why, I can't help but ask myself, would such a thing be sinful? After all, what son has not, at one time or another, seen his father naked?

Perhaps it was the *intent* that gave birth to the sinful behavior. Did Ham *want* to see his father naked? Of this, however, there is no allusion in the text.

Was Noah's nakedness, then, simply a metaphor, similar to Eve's apple, representing forbidden knowledge? Are there certain things that a son should never know of his father?

I stretch back in the chair, crossing my ankles, and fold my arms.

'Or of his grandfather?' I whisper.

Looking out the bedroom window into the clear, dark autumn sky, I listen to my father downstairs, clanging about in the kitchen.

Is he cooking something? I wonder.

Soon, I smell bacon frying.

'A father's duty,' I hear my grandfather say, 'is to provide his son with food, shelter, and an education in math, morality, and language. Anything more, or less, cannot be expected.'

'A son's duty,' he explains, 'is to be obedient and respectful. Do as I say, not as I do.'

Such simple definitions, I think: truthful in their essence, to be sure, but hardly considerate, much like the story of Noah and Ham, of all the variables innate in every father, every son—every man.

Suddenly, from downstairs, I hear my father call my name.

I stand, pushing back the chair, and leave the room. When he calls me, I have learned, I do not call in return; I go.

Downstairs in the kitchen, he is seated at the table, eating a sandwich. Behind him, in the shadowed living room, my grandfather is sleeping on the couch, snoring.

'Yes?' I say, looking at my father.

'I fried up some ham,' he replies, his mouth full. 'You want a sandwich?'

'No, thanks,' I answer.

'Suit yourself,' he says, shrugging and, though his mouth is full, taking another bite. His elbows resting on the table, he sits, chewing his food, and looks at me.

It is Baby's last night before leaving Essaouira. At YaYa's request, Maggie and I begrudgingly accompany the two of them for dinner at the restaurant where the four of us first met.

As before, the small, dark restaurant is crowded, noisy, thick with cigarette smoke and incense. We are given the same corner booth.

After eating, we once again remain at our table, talking, drinking red wine. Despite our full stomachs, the four of us are quickly inebriated. At the table next to ours is a rowdy group of Australian men, also drunk.

'How does such a small town get so many tourists?' YaYa remarks, glancing over his shoulder at the table of Australians.

'I guess they're here for the same reason we are,' Maggie offers, lighting yet another cigarette.

'Researching a book?' YaYa asks, smiling. 'I don't think so.'

'You never know,' Maggie replies.

'Escaping their past,' I suggest, winking at her.

'If they're from Australia,' she says, 'we can only hope so. Other than Americans, is there any group of people more obnoxious than Australians? With their sunburnt skin and vulgar—'

'I don't have a problem with them,' Baby interrupts, taking a sip of her wine.

Maggie looks at her.

It has been this way the entire evening. Maggie says something and Baby immediately disagrees.

'Then perhaps you should immigrate there,' Maggie replies, taking a drag of her cigarette and smiling.

'Maybe I will,' Baby says, apparently taking the suggestion seriously. 'But I have too much happening back home. How I was even able to get away for this trip, I'll never know. God.'

'Your little girlfriend bought your ticket, didn't she?' Maggie asks.

Baby looks at YaYa, not moving her head, then at Maggie.

Watching them, I suddenly feel a sharp pain, as if a knife, cut through my asshole up into my belly. Biting my lip, I close my eyes, and the pain abruptly vanishes.

'I bought it myself,' I hear Baby say sternly.

I open my eyes and look at her. Trembling, I place my hands on my thighs and take a deep, slow breath.

'Oh, I'm sorry,' Maggie replies, feigning embarrassment. 'I thought you said she had bought it for you; my mistake.'

Beneath the table, I bring my hands together. They are cold, damp.

'So,' YaYa suddenly says, 'do you think you'll ever come back to Morocco, Baby?'

She continues to look at Maggie, who returns her gaze, then turns to YaYa and smiles.

'Of course,' she says. 'But, you know, it's hard for me to get away.'

There is something she wants to tell us.

YaYa looks at Maggie, then at me, and says:

'Baby's a counselor; she works with homeless women. Plus, she volunteers twice a week at a suicide hotline. *And* she's about to make a documentary about—what is it about, again?'

'Prostitutes who were molested as children,' she replies sadly, yet proudly.

'Sounds interesting,' Maggie says, seeming genuinely interested, though I know she is not.

Baby looks at her, as if surprised, then says:

'Well, I hope it will be—if I can ever get the funding I need for it.'

Maggie shakes her head, frowning sympathetically.

'I got a grant from the NEA,' she explains, 'but it went for rent. Then I threw a big fundraising bash, but that went for rent, too. And lipstick.'

She laughs. It's hard not to like her when she laughs, I think.

'Are you going to be in the film yourself?' Maggie asks.

YaYa and I look at each other.

Behind him, two of the Australians are drinking wine straight from the bottle. One of them misses his mouth and the wine spills across his face, causing the others to erupt in laughter.

'I was thinking about it,' Baby replies, surprising me, 'but a few filmmakers I know said it's not such a good idea. So I doubt if I will. It's hard to be objective when you're both in front and behind of the camera, you know?'

'I can imagine,' Maggie agrees, again sympathetically.

Baby nods her head, drinking her wine. The three of us do the same.

'You know,' Baby then says, 'I was in a porno movie once. Can you believe it?'

'You're kidding!' Maggie exclaims, bumping her leg several times against mine.

Here we go, I think.

'I wish I was,' Baby replies, frowning, 'but I'm not. God, that was such an awful time in my life. But I needed the money, so I did it. You know?'

'I can imagine,' Maggie replies. 'You poor thing. Did you at least get paid well for it?'

YaYa looks at Maggie.

'Well,' Baby replies, appearing as if she is about to cry, 'I'd rather not talk about it. It's too—'

She begins to cry. Frowning, Maggie reaches forward and puts her hand on Baby's shoulder. Turning her head and looking at me, she says:

'I can imagine.'

I notice that Baby cries without sound or tears. Eyes closed, she holds her hands to her mouth, silently, softly rocking back and forth in her seat.

Suddenly, inexplicably, I hate her.

When Baby, dabbing her dry eyes with a napkin, excuses herself from the table to use the restroom, I turn in my seat and look at Maggie.

'Go ahead,' I say.

'Go ahead what?'

'Go ahead,' I repeat. 'I can't wait to hear what you have to say this time.'

Adjusting the straps of her long black dress, she looks at me, then at YaYa, and smiles mischievously.

'For your information,' she says, 'I've grown quite fond of Baby.'

'Oh, really?'

'Really.'

'I can tell,' YaYa says, looking at her, 'by your interest in her life and—and how you're able to ask just the right questions and—'

'Well,' she interrupts, 'what good is she for if not her disgusting little stories? They're about as—oh, and why, after all she's told us, would some porno movie she's supposedly been in make her cry? Please.'

'Everything that bothers you,' YaYa offers, 'bothers you equally?'

'No,' Maggie replies, 'but a gunshot to the left probably wouldn't matter more than a gunshot to the right. And other than a trip to Sunday school, I seriously doubt that there's too much that can make that bitch cry. Please. She didn't even have any tears.'

'Has anyone ever told you,' YaYa says, 'that *you're* a bitch?'

I look at him. Though he is smiling, he is obviously angry.

'Sweetie,' Maggie replies, either missing or ignoring his

anger, 'of course they have. But let me say this, in my defense, brother: I have no qualms giving people what they secretly, and sometimes not so secretly, want.'

'What the hell does that mean?' YaYa asks.

'What it means,' Maggie explains, leaning forward, 'is that Baby is a perpetual victim. I've seen her type a thousand times. Being a victim has ennobled her in a way that nothing else ever could. Hell, if it's all too painful to discuss then why does she bring it up? I'll tell you why—because her B-movie mistakes give her a depth, a *sense* of depth, that she just doesn't have. Suicide hotline? Please. Suffering is what gives her *life*.'

'Perhaps,' YaYa says, looking at her. 'But—'

He is silent for a moment.

'But I like her,' he continues. 'Kind of.'

'Of course you like her,' Maggie says, laughing loudly. 'You're a goddamned writer; you writers *adore* fucked-up bitches like her. It's the ones who have their acts together, like me, of course, that bore you. Besides, she's probably a nasty bitch in bed, and a man doesn't have to be a writer to enjoy that. Now does he?'

She giggles, batting her eyelashes at him. He shrugs.

'Besides,' Maggie continues, 'I'm sure you'll write all about her one of these days. Isn't that what you writers do: take the misery of others and turn it into a little morality tale? A little *lesson?*'

'What's worse,' YaYa asks, 'that or laughing about it? Making light of it?'

'I never laughed about it,' she replies, 'but you did.'

'I did not,' YaYa replies.

'Yes,' Maggie says, 'you did. In fact, you couldn't stop laughing. Remember? When she left to use the washroom the night we met?'

YaYa is silent for a moment, then replies:

'I was laughing at you and what you were saying, not at her.'

'Oh,' Maggie counters facetiously, 'I see.'

Frowning, she takes a sip of her wine and continues:

'Nonetheless, I—yes, I did make light of it. And I don't apologize for that. She makes me—she irritates me. With her tall tales and verbal crotch-baring. It's humiliating. She humiliates herself. And all women, she humiliates us all. Especially black women.'

'I thought you were growing fond of her,' I say.

She looks at me.

'I am,' she says, smiling. 'I can honestly say that I will miss her when she leaves tomorrow.'

'I'm sure you will,' offers YaYa, looking skeptically at Maggie. She winks at him.

We are silent for a moment, looking at one another. Maggie takes a sip of her wine, then lights a cigarette.

'Are there any nightclubs in this wretched town?' she suddenly asks, setting the cigarette on the ashtray's glass lip. 'I feel like dancing.'

'You are dancing,' YaYa says, drinking his wine.

Baby returns from the restroom, smiling, and sits down, putting her purse beside her.

'Sorry, folks,' she says, looking at Maggie, who ignores her.

'She wants to go dancing,' I say to Baby. 'Do you know anywhere we can go dancing? I don't.'

'That's the most I've heard you say all night,' Maggie says, turning toward me.

'I've just been listening,' I explain, 'to all the fascinating conversation.'

'Oh,' she exclaims, 'you can hear what they're saying in the kitchen?'

YaYa frowns.

'Anyway,' Maggie says, looking at Baby, 'do you know anyplace we can dance? Outside of the Medina, in the new part, maybe?'

'No, I don't,' Baby answers, shaking her head.

'We could go to that bar by the beach,' YaYa suggests. 'There's no dancefloor, but there's music.'

'Well,' Maggie replies, 'do you folks want to go? I do.'

Before anyone can answer, she picks up her purse, puts it over her shoulder, and stands. She then waves at the waiter, calling him to our table.

Later that night in my hotel room, Maggie and I lie in bed talking. She informs me, as if suddenly remembering, that she has recently talked with Jonathan; he will be arriving in Essaouira the day after tomorrow. In less than a week, she explains, the two of them will be returning to Paris, then to New York City.

After a moment of silence, I inform her that I, too, will soon be leaving Morocco. Perhaps, I suggest, we can meet in New York before I return to the farm.

'Why the hell are you going back to the farm?' she asks, raising her head off my chest and looking at me. Her breath has the faint smell of semen.

'Maggie,' I reply, 'why do you think?'

'To drive yourself mad,' she says, returning her head to my chest and rubbing my belly with her hand. 'Or should I say madder?'

'Well,' I say, 'besides that, there are the—the legal matters. I mean, I have to put the farm up for sale; I can't just leave it there. I was thinking I'd probably keep the house and just sell the land.'

'Why would you keep the house?' she asks, running her hand along my side and up to my armpit, where she gently pulls at my underarm hair.

'I don't know,' I reply, looking up at the darkened ceiling. 'Maybe I'll retire there one day.'

'Do you think you'll ever want—'

She pauses for a moment and then resumes.

'I was about to say chickens. Do you think you'll ever want *children?*'

'Never,' I reply. 'I never want children.'

'Alright,' she giggles. 'You don't have to scream.'

I rub her bare shoulder, then kiss the top of her head.

'Do you want children?' I ask.

'Never,' she replies, mimicking me. 'I never want children. Or chickens.'

She turns and looks up at the ceiling.

'I hate them,' she says, becoming suddenly still. 'Well, I don't hate them, but I certainly don't want one either. If I could somehow give birth to a sixteen-year-old, then maybe, but when they're little, I just—I just can't relate to them. I don't know how to *talk* to them. They're like little aliens or—or cockroaches.'

I pull her close.

'Cockroaches,' I laugh. 'You're mean.'

'Maybe,' she replies, giggling again. 'But better I'm mean and childless than mean and—and trying to raise some little creature I can't even relate to. Right?'

'Right,' I agree.

The next day, after accompanying Baby to the bus depot, Maggie and I go for lunch with YaYa, then for a walk. YaYa, looking slightly forlorn, returns to the hotel to write.

'I miss Baby already,' Maggie says, stopping to look at a sidewalk vendor's array of small, Thuja boxes. The vendor, an elderly man with brown skin and a white beard, looks at us but says nothing.

'Oh, do you now?' I ask.

I watch her as she delicately fingers one of the small pearl-inlaid boxes.

'One of my guiding principles in life,' she says, turning toward me, 'is to have as—'

She stops, turning back to the vendor.

'*Shukran,*' she says, smiling.

'*La shukran Allah wajib,*' he replies, smiling in return.

'As I was saying,' she says, taking my hand and beginning to walk again, 'one of my greatest goals in life is to become friends with as many people as possible that I hate.'

'Thanks a lot,' I say.

'But not you, of course,' she laughs.

'Of course not,' I say, squeezing her hand in mine.

'I mean, why do we usually dislike someone? Because of how they make us feel when we're around them. Right?'

'Usually,' I agree, watching as two women, both shrouded entirely in black, walk slowly toward us, then pass.

'And if someone makes me uncomfortable,' Maggie continues, 'then I have to ask myself why. And the reason usually has more to do with me than it does with the other person. I'm not talking about someone who sneaks money out of my purse or—or burns my neck with a lit cigarette. It's obvious why I wouldn't like them. But then there are the others, those who are boorish or ignorant or obnoxiously loud, or maybe one of those people I seem to dislike for no particular reason—people whose behavior usually does not directly effect my own. Like with Baby. I have to ask myself why I dislike such people. It sometimes seems obvious, and maybe it is. But why, really, should they bother me even one whit? They're not paying my rent, right? And to become friends with such people, to understand them, can only *benefit* me. What I want—what I ultimately want—is to reach the point where absolutely no one has the power to even remotely irritate me. No one. *That's* freedom. Strength. And I want it.'

'Hey,' I say, 'I want that, too. Doesn't everyone?'

'In theory, maybe, but few people do anything to actually achieve it. Most people are friendly only with those who are similar to themselves. Right? Who agree with the choices they make, have made. Seems like what most people really want is just a rose-tinted mirror. Nobody wants to ask any fucking questions, or to be asked any. And, besides, *you* are already like that. Nothing bothers you. Well, other than when you—when you break down.'

'Oh, really,' I reply, looking down at her.

'Maybe you're just an expert, like you say, at compartmentalizing things. But you're certainly the most laid-back brother I've ever known. Deadpan, I think, is the word. Even when you're angry.'

'I prefer *smooth*,' I reply, smiling.

'I'm sure you do,' she says, stopping to look in the grimy window of a small, cluttered bookstore.

'Isn't Arabic script beautiful?' she asks. 'Each letter is a tiny work of art. A short story.'

I nod my head, looking through the opened doorway into the shadowed, dusty bookstore. A small, thin man behind the counter looks up at me.

'*A salaam aleikum,*' he calls out, smiling.

'*Aleikum salaam,*' I reply, waving my hand at him.

Though I am aware of the pain, it is an intellectual awareness that causes me, simply, to think:

This hurts.

Holding onto either side of the bathtub, I slowly lower myself into the warm water. I take a deep breath, closing my eyes, then opening them. The water begins to turn pink.

I rest slowly on the bottom of the tub; leaning back, I raise my legs out of the water. Trembling, I take the dry blue bar of soap, dip it into the water, and begin to lather it between my hands. As I do this, without expression or sound, I begin to cry.

Folding my clothes and passing them to the attendant, I am aware of those behind me, dressing or undressing, watching me. Is it because I am black, I wonder, or simply because I am a foreigner?

I turn and discover that none of the ten to twelve men behind me are looking at me. I walk quickly past them and, opening the heavy, wooden door, enter the darkened, steaming chambers of the hammam.

Though it is crowded, there is little noise: wet feet across the stone floor, whispered intonations of praying men, and the steady, rhythmic sound of water pouring, splashing, dripping.

In each of the several low-ceilinged rooms is a single, low-watt bulb that illuminates little more than itself. A heavy, hot steam hangs in the air.

Finding a vacant spot in one of the room's corners, I sit, cross-legged, on the warm floor and lean against the wet stone wall. YaYa and I have smoked a joint just minutes before, and I am stoned. I close my eyes, my head spinning, and listen to the hypnotic rhythm of sound.

Next to me, I hear a man whispering:

'*Bismallah a rahman a rahim.*'

I open my eyes and look at him without moving my head. He is about my age, with a slender build, pale skin, and short, curly black hair. Facing the wall, his legs spread, he looks down, trimming his pubic hair with a small pair of scissors.

Across from me, nearly invisible in the steam, I see a hairy-backed man wearing red jockey shorts, pouring a metal bucket of water over his head. The cold water splashes me as it hits the floor.

Leaning my head against the stone wall, I look up into the shadowed, rolling clouds of steam. As the sweat begins to form, then roll down my back and chest and belly, I uncross my legs and rest my elbows on my knees; my hands hang limp. Soon, my boxer shorts are soaked and sweat drips slowly from my fingertips.

I close my eyes, thinking about Maggie, about my father, about everything that needs to be done upon returning to America. I think of a choreographer I once knew, briefly. I think of Jonathan and Baby and YaYa. He said he would meet me here, and I wonder if he will come.

A naked man walks by, steps on my toes, and continues walking. An extremely old man, bearded, gaunt, hunchbacked, walks slowly by. In his hand is a wet towel that he drags along the floor. Behind him is a boy of twelve or thirteen, carrying a bar of soap and a pocket knife. Next to me, on the opposite side of the man trimming his pubic hair, I notice YaYa; he sits quietly, looking at me.

'When the hell did you get here?' I whisper, leaning toward him.

'When did I get here?' he replies, also whispering. 'Motherfucker, I came in with you.'

Laughing softly, nearly inaudibly, I lower my head, looking down at the wet, stone floor between my legs.

'Brother, brother,' YaYa whispers, 'you need to get a *grip.*'

'Forget Pip,' I reply, looking up at him. 'Who the hell is Pip?'

YaYa raises a fist to his mouth, attempting to stifle a laugh.

'I said you need to get a *grip,*' he says, looking at me. 'Now be quiet; you'll get us both kicked out of here.'

My head still lowered, I close my eyes.

'Did you bring any soap?' I ask.

Feeling something touch my thigh, I open my eyes; in YaYa's hand is an unused bar of white soap.

'Thanks,' I whisper, raising my hand and taking the soap.

Struggling to my feet, I put my free hand on YaYa's shoulder and whisper:

'Come on; help me.'

Shuffling into the adjacent room, stepping over several men lying prone on the floor, I stand next to a group of men hovering next to one of the two rusted metal taps that jut from the stone wall.

On the floor next to the tap is an empty plastic bucket. I turn on the tap, filling the bucket with water, and ask YaYa to pour it over my back and head.

'Yes, Massa,' he replies, picking up the bucket and slowly pouring the nearly scalding water over my head. As he does this, I lather my body with soap.

Refilling the bucket, YaYa again slowly pours it over my head. Once I'm completely rinsed, I step aside.

'Your turn,' I say to YaYa, squatting next to the tap and filling it again with water.

As I do this, I notice suddenly that he is naked and that his cock is as small as a child's.

'You're supposed to wear underwear in a hammam, YaYa,' I say, standing, then pouring the water slowly over his head and shoulders.

'I've seen a few guys without any,' he replies, shrugging, as he lathers the soap across his chest.

I close my eyes.

You're lucky it's so small, I think. Otherwise, you'd have to—

Suddenly, the bucket slips from my hands and falls to the floor. Opening my eyes, I pick up the bucket and again fill it with water.

Once done, YaYa and I return to the previous room. Our places have been taken, and we turn and walk through the steam into another, less crowded room. Finding space, we sit on the floor, resting our backs against the wall. Silently, we each stare into the shadows, lost in our private thoughts.

It is, I think, as if YaYa has become someone, something different, his tiny penis a reflection of another hidden attribute, another fault. I am almost *angry* with him.

I am reminded of my recent conversation with Maggie. What, I wonder, does my uneasiness about YaYa, and what is between his legs, say about *me?*

The obvious conclusion, of course, would be that I am insecure about my own endowment, my own masculinity, but such a suggestion seems inappropriate; the size of my cock, while oft considered, has never, personally, been much cause for concern, or worry.

I look into the shifting mass of men as they drift in and out of the clouds of steam. Some sit; some stand; some kneel. A small boy, no older than five, runs by; a man I presume to be his father chases after him.

I turn to look at YaYa. His eyes are closed. He leans forward, head bowed, with his hands resting on his outstretched legs. Fastened with a white ribbon, his dreadlocks hang wet across his back.

Glancing quickly between his legs, I look at the shadowed outline of his penis, then close my eyes.

Suddenly, I remember my father, naked, dead, lying on his bed. The thought startles me and I push it from my mind. Then, I remember my grandfather. I see his face, emotionless, stoic, staring at me from a darkened doorway.

'A father's duty,' I hear him say, 'is to provide his son with food, shelter, and an education in math, morality, and language.'

'And a son's duty,' I hear my father say, 'is to be obedient and respectful.'

I open my eyes, trembling, and look down between my legs. I am, I suddenly realize, slowly but steadily pissing onto the warm, stone floor.

Pulling the bloodied sheets from my bed, I roll them into a tight ball and walk to the closet. Opening it, I look inside and drop the sheets on the floor.

Closing the door, I turn, looking at the bare blue-and-white-striped mattress. At its center is a light brown stain. I walk to the bed, throwing the pillows on the floor, and turn the mattress over.

At its center is a large, dark yellow stain.

What, I wonder, do I prefer: a yellow stain or a brown stain? Brown indicates blood or shit. Yellow would be piss or maybe semen.

Sitting on the edge of the bed, I look at the bedroom door; it is closed, locked.

A brown stain, I think. I would prefer a brown stain.

Leaning forward, I clutch the side of the bed and vomit onto the floor.

I do not go with Maggie to the bus depot for Jonathan's arrival. Instead, I jog along the beach, stopping occasionally, lost in thought. It is a cool day, windy, and the sky is overcast.

Hearing someone behind me, I glance over my shoulder, continuing to jog. No one is there. I stop and turn toward the ocean. I stretch from side to side, then bend forward, my legs straight, and touch the wet sand. Rising, I bring my feet together and, counting aloud, do two hundred jumping jacks.

After I've finished, I again bend forward and touch the sand with the palms of my hands. In this position, I slowly count from one to twenty, then rise, looking out across the calm blue water. Far in the distance, I see several small wooden fishing boats.

In one of the boats, I see someone standing, waving. I watch the figure, curious, and wave in return.

Returning to the hotel, I see YaYa at one of the café's outdoor tables. Huddled over, pen in hand, he writes quickly on a yellow pad of legal paper. Not wanting to interrupt his work, I enter the hotel without greeting him.

After showering, I return to my room and begin to dress. From the room next to mine, I hear what sounds like a small dog barking. Standing still, my underwear in my hand, I look at the cracked, bluish-white wall that separates the two rooms. Abruptly, the barking stops.

Was it a dog? I wonder, slipping on my underwear.

Noticing a plastic bottle of lotion on the shelf above the sink, I slip off my underwear and cover my entire body, from skull to sole, with lotion, massaging it into my skin with firm, circular strokes. As I do this, I feel a large, callused hand touch my back. I ignore it. Finished, I again slip on my underwear, then wash my hands.

In my underwear, I stretch across the bed, fold my hands on my belly, and close my eyes. I am suddenly, inexplicably, depressed.

Turning on my side, resting my hands between my thighs, I count backwards from one hundred, stopping at thirty-seven. Opening my eyes, I stare at the wall and count aloud back up to one hundred.

Later that afternoon, Maggie returns to find me in bed, still in my underwear, sleeping. Closing the door behind her, she crawls into bed and puts her arm around my chest.

'Where's John-boy?' I ask, turning slowly in the bed to face her.

'In his room,' she replies, 'taking a shower.'

'He has his own shower?'

She giggles, kissing me on the chin. She smells, I think, like a cucumber.

'And a terrace,' she says, smiling at me.

'A life of luxury, huh?'

'Well, he wanted to stay in my room but I told him he couldn't. Then he was convinced I was staying in your room, and he wouldn't believe otherwise. So I told him to fuck off—and I left. But I told him we'd meet him for dinner. Do you mind?'

'He's not going to beat me up,' I ask, 'is he?'

She giggles.

'Well, don't worry,' she says, 'I'll protect you.'

'Please do,' I reply, leaning forward and running my tongue between her lips, opening them.

Though she insists I get out of bed, I manage with little effort to convince her to take off her panties and sit with her legs spread on my chest.

'I missed it,' I whisper, staring between her smooth, dark thighs.

'I'm sure you did,' she replies, looking down at me as she puts one hand on either side of my face.

Later that evening, Maggie, Jonathan, and I return to our restaurant of choice. YaYa was invited, but explained that he was too busy writing. He would, perhaps, meet us later.

Though the evening begins pleasantly, with the three of us eating, drinking, and talking as friends, I soon notice, when watching Jonathan, a slight uneasiness, even anger. Occasionally, he will look at me, and at Maggie, from narrowed, suspicious eyes; his words, however, remain polite, friendly, even humorous.

Rolling the sleeves of his pale blue, button-down shirt to his elbows, as if he's about to fight, he tells us of his time alone in Tangier and of his plans for Maggie and himself in Paris. Maggie frowns, but remains silent.

He reminds me of a polo player or television anchorman: the photogenic, clean-shaven face, bright blue eyes, and perfect teeth.

'You had Abderahim very worried,' he says, looking at me. 'He was positive you were crazy.'

'Yes, well,' I reply, slightly embarrassed, 'he's quite perceptive, isn't he?'

'So you are crazy, then?' Jonathan says, smiling at me as if I am a waiter and he is the customer.

'Indeed I am,' I reply. 'Didn't Maggie tell you?'

'Well,' he says, chuckling, 'she told me you killed your father.'

Maggie turns to me, but I do not look at her.

'Oh, did she now?'

'That first night,' I hear Maggie say, 'I told him. But that was before I really—'

Ignoring her, I take a sip of wine and watch Jonathan.

'And you believed her?' I ask.

'Well,' he replies, 'I believe that you said it to her.'

'But do you believe I did it?'

'I don't know you well enough to say. It's possible. But I doubt if someone who actually did such a thing would go around telling strangers. Either way, to say such a thing, true or not, *is* rather crazy.'

'If I did it,' I say, 'but didn't tell anyone about it, would I still be crazy?'

'Marvin Gay killed his son,' Jonathan replies. 'Was he crazy?'

'Marvin Gaye didn't kill his son,' Maggie says. 'He was killed by his father.'

'I know,' Jonathan says. 'There was a junior and a senior; Marvin Gay, without the *e*, killed his son, Marvin Gaye, with the *e*. He added the *e* himself. Senior killed junior. It was the—'

'Okay,' Maggie interrupts, 'we get the picture.'

'Well,' Jonathan asks me, 'was he crazy?'

'I have no idea,' I answer. 'Maybe he just got to the gun first.'

'Perhaps,' Jonathan says.

'If I did do it,' I ask, 'and could prove it, what would you do?'

'What could I do?'

'Make a citizen's arrest,' I reply.

Maggie giggles.

'Who would care here in Morocco?' he asks.

'Well,' I reply, 'when you get back to the States, you could find someone, I'm sure, who would care.'

'Well,' he says, smiling, 'if the police ever come looking for me, I'll tell them. Otherwise, your secret is safe with me.'

'Good, I wouldn't want to have to kill you, too.'

Maggie laughs; Jonathan does not. Instead, he takes a drink of wine, his eyes fixed on me, and smiles.

'I wouldn't want that, either,' he replies.

The three of us are silent, watching one another.

'Well,' Maggie eventually says, 'there are certainly a lot of people I'd *like* to kill.'

Jonathan looks at her, frowning; he is certain, I can tell, that she is referring to him.

'I don't know if I'd be able to stab them,' she continues, 'or strangle them. But I'd be able to shoot them; that's for sure. And I could probably run them over with a car, or poison them, but if I poisoned them, I wouldn't want to have to watch them die, you know?'

She lights a cigarette, looking over Jonathan's shoulder.

'I could kill my father,' she says, glancing at me. 'I could kill my oldest brother, Norbert, too, and I could kill the Pope. I could kill Steven Spielberg and—and Oprah Winfrey. I could kill the noisy bitch who lives in the apartment next to mine. I could kill, you know, I could walk into a bank and shoot every last one of the tellers.'

Jonathan and I sit silently, listening to Maggie.

'Who else could I kill?' she continues. 'There are a few teachers from where I went to school that I could kill. Mr. Collis. Mrs. Zyla. Mrs. Tompkins. The principal. What was his name? He'd be the first one I'd kill. I might even be able to *strangle* him.'

'That's quite a list,' Jonathan remarks. 'Did you smoke a joint before we came here?'

'No, asshole, I didn't,' she lies, taking a drag of her cigarette and blowing the smoke in his face.

'Who could you kill?' I ask Jonathan, watching him fan the smoke with his hand, frowning.

'Oh, please!' Maggie exclaims. 'He couldn't kill anyone.'

Jonathan looks at her.

'That's not a bad thing, Maggie,' he says.

'Yes,' she replies, 'it is. I could never trust a man who was incapable of killing.'

'Killing what?' Jonathan asks.

'Another man,' she replies.

'Are you serious?' he asks. 'Well, you must not trust me then.'

'Let me put it this way, Jonathan,' she says. 'I don't trust you. I think you could possibly kill a man, so that's not the reason. But just because I couldn't trust a man incapable of killing doesn't mean I trust every man who *is* capable of it.'

'You don't trust me?' Jonathan asks, apparently offended.

'I'm not talking about murder for the sake of murder,' Maggie says, ignoring Jonathan's question. 'I'm talking about— about a variety of circumstances in which the death of one man, or woman, would result in a substantial benefit to others.'

Listening to her, I am drawn to the elaborate necklace around her neck. Made of pine nuts, silver beads, and porcupine quills, it catches the reflection of the candle flame, glittering as she moves in her seat.

'I thought you were against capital punishment,' Jonathan offers.

'I am,' she replies, 'wholeheartedly. What I'm talking about is bigger than revenge. Bigger than—you know, there's this misperception that we, black people, are violent, but if we were even half as violent as white folks believe, they'd all be dead. Piles of bodies, everywhere.'

I look at her face.

Instead, I think, we kill each other.

'It would be a whole different world,' she says, 'if we had done what we were justified to do.'

She looks at me, then at Jonathan.

'Malcolm knew the score,' she continues. 'The ballot or the

bullet. By any means necessary. There can be no revolution without bloodshed.'

'He disavowed many of his beliefs before he died,' Jonathan says.

'He *expanded* many of his beliefs,' Maggie says. 'There's a difference.'

Jonathan shrugs, looking down at the table, as if somehow embarrassed.

'The problem with this world,' Maggie says, 'is that all the wrong people have been doing the killing.'

'That should tell you something about killing,' Jonathan replies.

'Maybe,' Maggie agrees. 'But it also tells me just as much about those who aren't doing it.'

'And what is that?' Jonathan asks. 'That we're cowards?'

'Some of us but not all of us. My only point, dear Jonathan, is that this world would be a better place to live if some of us could learn how to shoot a gun.'

'You can be very unlikable sometimes, Maggie,' Jonathan says. 'Do you know that?'

He shakes his head in disgust.

'Oh, Johnny,' Maggie says, reaching across the table and touching his cheek, 'don't be so hateful. I'm just playing with you.'

'And now you double-clutch,' he says.

'I'm not double-clutching,' she replies. 'I'm just trying to look at certain things from different perspectives. I *could* kill someone, but I doubt if I ever would. I'm a coward, too.'

Maggie looks at me and winks.

'Well,' Jonathan says, looking up, 'I guess there's a few people I could kill.'

'There you go,' Maggie replies, laughing heartily. 'Good for you!'

As we continue talking, I notice that Jonathan is no longer uneasy. Maggie's attention and humor, it seems, have somehow calmed him.

Still, I occasionally notice the two of them looking at one another as if in collusion: a raised eyebrow or sudden shift of attention, lowered eyelids, a slight smile or frown. More than once, Jonathan begins to say something but, glancing at Maggie, abruptly stops.

Listening to them talk, I look up at the door and watch as an older black gentleman walks in and, after talking briefly with the waiter, is seated at a nearby table.

The man is tall and thin, very dark, wearing a white two-piece suit, white shirt, and bright green tie. His hair is cropped close to his head, perfectly silver. There is an elegance, a sophistication, to his demeanor and dress that reminds me of a professor or, perhaps, a political dignitary.

If he is a teacher, I wonder, what would he teach: literature, perhaps *French* literature, or philosophy?

'Who, my dear, are you staring at?' I hear Maggie ask. She looks at me, then around the crowded restaurant.

'That man by the door,' I reply. 'The ambassador.'

'Ambassador?'

Jonathan turns, looking behind him. As he does this, I notice a small, round sore, like a fresh burn, at the nape of his neck.

'The guy with the green tie?' he asks. 'He's an ambassador? To where?'

'Well,' I reply, staring at his neck, 'I don't know if he's an ambassador. I was just trying to imagine what his story was—is.'

'Why?' Jonathan asks, turning forward in his seat and looking at me. As he turns, the sore at the nape of his neck becomes hidden beneath his collar. Wondering briefly of its origin, I look at his face.

'I don't know,' I reply. 'It's—it's not too often I see a man in an all-white suit and bright green tie.'

'Very elegant,' Maggie says, drinking from her glass of wine. 'He's gorgeous.'

'Gorgeous?' Jonathan asks.

'Yes,' she replies, 'gorgeous. He has to be African; Westerners are too ashamed of themselves to dress so—so gorgeously. Except for American Indians, of course. Is there any traditional dress more beautiful than theirs? There isn't. It almost makes me cry when I think of how beautiful it is.'

'What about the Dutch?' I ask.

Maggie leans back in her chair, laughing.

'With their little wooden shoes,' she says, giggling. 'And Pippi Longstocking braids!'

'Do you remember,' Jonathan begins, 'when we were—'

Suddenly, looking at Maggie, he stops.

'Remember what?' she asks him.

'Nothing,' he replies.

'Yes,' Maggie says, 'I remember nothing. Do you?'

'Very well,' he answers.

'Me, too,' I add, watching them look at each other, then look away.

Surprising me, my father offers me a ride to the bus depot. Our drive into town is silent, each of us staring out into the countryside. I am anxious, even a bit frightened. Most of all, I am relieved. By tomorrow evening I will be in New York City. What, I wonder, will happen?

In the bus depot's parking lot, my father steers the pickup into a vacant space and turns off the ignition. His hands on the steering wheel as if he is anxious to leave, he stares at the rusted Cadillac parked ahead of us.

'You know, Dad,' I say, 'you don't have to come in with me. You have—you have a long drive home, and there's still a half hour before my bus leaves. I'll just get a coffee or something.'

Taking an envelope from his shirt pocket, he folds it in half and passes it to me, still looking at the Cadillac.

'Put this in your bag there,' he says.

Silently, I take the envelope and, leaning forward, slip it in the side of my knapsack on the truck's floor.

Is it a letter? I wonder. I hope not.

I sit straight and look out the window at the bus depot's entrance. Two young Asian girls walk inside, each lugging a huge backpack. Behind them is a skinny, teenaged white boy with long, blond hair, tight blue jeans, and huge, white sneakers. On the back of his black T-shirt are the words, *'Get in the Ring, Motherfucker.'*

I turn to my father.

'Well, son,' he says, 'you better get going.'

Looking at me, he holds out his huge hand. I shake it at once, then reach forward and pick up my knapsack.

'If you get into trouble,' he says, 'call me.'

'I will,' I say, opening the truck door and stepping out onto the pavement.

No, I think, I won't.

Taking my suitcase from the back of the truck, I stand for a second and look at my father.

'Goodbye, Dad,' I say.

'Okay, then,' he replies, starting the ignition.

I shut the truck's door and watch through the passenger's window as my father shifts into gear. No longer looking at me, he steers the old truck backwards and out of the parking lot.

As I sit in the waiting area at the depot, I take the envelope from my knapsack and open it. Inside are fifteen one-hundred-dollar bills.

When Maggie informs me that she and Jonathan will be travelling to Agadir for two days, I am neither surprised nor upset.

'But don't freak out and run off this time,' she says, kissing me. 'We'll be back. Okay?'

'Okay,' I reply.

'You're not pissed off,' she asks, 'are you?'

'Why would I be pissed off?' I reply. 'You're not my wife. I don't even know your last name.'

'You're pissed off.'

Putting a hand on either side of her head, I raise her face to mine.

'I'm not pissed off,' I say. 'You two came to Morocco together, and I'm sure he's been lonely this last week without you. Go on; enjoy yourselves.'

She looks up at me, a bit suspiciously, then smiles.

'Well, I definitely won't enjoy myself,' she says, again kissing me, 'but I'll try, at least, not to kill myself.'

'Or Jonathan,' I reply.

'That I can't promise.'

Delicately, slowly, she begins to unbutton my shirt, kissing me.

'Walker,' she whispers.

'What?' I ask, putting my hands to her breasts.

'My last name is Walker.'

Later that evening, I sit with YaYa at the café next to our hotel. As he writes, I sip my tea and watch the people around me.

It is a warm night with a clear sky; though there are few tourists, the street is busy, noisy. Oddly, however, there are few people seated at the café's tables: five, including YaYa and me.

The middle-aged American woman returns, still wearing a dirty blue djellaba and carrying her large, straw purse, and again asks the waiter for bones. As before, he gives her a plastic bag, filled, and the woman thanks him and quickly walks away.

I look at YaYa, but he is immersed in what he is writing, his hand scribbling quickly across the lined, yellow paper.

Over the next hour, I am approached by two boys and a girl, each offering shoe shines. I decline them all. Two teenaged boys I have never seen before ask to borrow ten dirham. I give it to them.

An elderly veiled woman sells me a copper bracelet and a carved wooden ring for five American dollars. A young man resembling Mussolini suggests we go for a walk along the beach. A long walk, he explains.

'One hundred dirham,' he says, smiling. His teeth are jagged, rotting.

'For what?' I ask.

'A walk. You know.'

'Get lost,' I tell him.

As he leaves, YaYa looks up from his writing and laughs.

'You're popular,' he says.

'Must be my peaceful disposition,' I reply, sucking air through my teeth. 'Damn.'

'Must be,' he chuckles, as he returns to his writing.

I begin to count the people passing by, one by one, until I reach forty-two. Turning to YaYa, I ask if he would like to accompany me to the hammam. As I ask this, I am reminded suddenly of his tiny, uncircumcised penis.

'Hey, man,' he says, looking up, 'I'm still trying to gain back the twelve pounds I sweated out last time we were there. Besides, that place gives me the willies. I kept expecting someone to walk by in shackles.'

'Well,' I say, 'I'm going to head over there. I'll see you later, bro.'

'Later,' he says, returning to his writing.

Though there are several men in the changing area, the hammam itself is empty. Having smoked half of a joint on my way over, I wander, mildly stoned, through the shadowed, steam-filled rooms and settle finally in the darkest corner.

Legs cocked, I rest my elbows on my knees, the palms of my hands turned upward, and stare into the swirling, shadowed clouds of steam. Soon, I am dripping with sweat; since no one is around, I raise my ass off the floor and slip out of my underwear, dropping them in a wet pile next to my shaving kit.

Lowering my head, I rest my chin on my chest and close my eyes. Though it is not yet nine o'clock, I am dazed, sleepy; the heat, steam, and drug-induced haze converge to pull me, as if weighted, into a near delirium.

Slowly, I open my eyes and raise my head. I look to my left, to my right, and then straight ahead. If I think of anything, it is of the need to think nothing, aware of only that which is before me.

I sit straight, overwhelmed by a sudden déjà vu. Closing my eyes, I raise my hands, covering my face, and try to prolong the sense, to—to *stretch* it into something tangible, something precise.

If I think of anything it is of the need to think nothing, aware of only that which is before me.

Opening my eyes, I lower my hands, telling myself to *remember*. I do not. I cannot.

Abruptly, the sensation vanishes, is pulled back into the shadows around me. Frustrated, I again raise my arms, roughly rubbing my forehead with the palms of my hands.

'*Bonsoir,*' I hear a man say.

Startled, I look up into the shadows but see no one, nothing.

'*Comme ça va?*' the voice asks. '*Et tu malade?*'

'Who's there?' I ask, leaning forward, peering into the rolling clouds of steam.

'You speak English,' the voice says. 'Good.'

Slowly, as if born of the steam itself, a man steps out of the shadows. I realize it is the tall, silver-haired gentleman from the restaurant. He is wearing a blood-red towel around his waist and, on his feet, a pair of black, plastic sandals.

'Oh,' I say, suddenly aware of my nakedness. 'Hello. Good evening.'

His name, he says, is Abayomi.

Stretching forward, I extend my hand. He shakes it firmly. I fold my hands, then rest them in my lap. I am, I realize, ashamed. I am ashamed in his presence.

'Are you alright, son?' he asks, standing, looking down at me.

'Oh, yeah,' I reply. 'Yeah. I was just—just thinking.'

'Unpleasant thoughts, I presume?'

His voice is deep, steady, with a slight trace of Nigerian, I think, in its rhythm.

'Well, you know, Abayomi,' I reply, looking up at him, 'if a man thinks enough, he'll eventually get to the unpleasant thoughts. Right?'

'Indeed,' he says, laughing softly.

I watch him as he slowly moves to my left, perhaps two feet, three feet away, and sits on the floor. Judging by his deliberate movements, he is older than his appearance would imply: sixty-five, perhaps, even seventy.

'Do you mind if I sit here?' he asks, crossing his legs.

Hanging from a leather strap around his neck is a round, jade pendant. Though I would prefer to be alone, I look at his face and reply:

'Of course not.'

'You were in that restaurant a couple of nights ago,' he says, looking at me. 'Yes?'

'Yes,' I reply, 'I was.'

'With your beautiful friend and a Jewish fellow,' he says. 'The three of you were looking at me. Watching me.'

'Oh,' I reply, nodding my head. 'We were trying to figure out what—what your story was. My guess was an ambassador or professor. Maggie figured you were African—and fabulous. She said you were gorgeous.'

Though I expect him to react to Maggie's compliment, he says instead:

'You were correct, my brother; I am a professor at the Sorbonne in Paris. Tell your friend that she, too, was correct. About my being from Africa, anyway.'

He laughs softly.

I look at him, then down at my lap, ensuring that my cock and balls are hidden beneath my hands. I want to take my wet underwear and slip them on, but I do not want him to see me do so. I sit still, quiet, staring into the shadows.

His hands rest on his knees, and he, too, is silent. Eyes closed, he breathes slowly, deeply, his narrow, muscled chest and belly rising, falling. Like my father and grandfather, I note, he is the color of eggplant.

'Not an ounce of the white man's blood,' my grandfather often claimed.

'Until you,' he would add, looking at my dark brown skin, and frowning.

'She wasn't white,' my father once said, referring to my mother.

'She was a Plains Cree Indian from Canada.'

'Well, she had white in her,' my grandfather replied, 'like most Indians.'

Ensuring that Abayomi's eyes are closed, I reach for my underwear. Standing slowly, wobbling on one foot, then the other, I slip them on. Feeling as if I am about to faint, I quickly squat and, turning, fall back on my ass.

Abayomi opens his eyes, looks at me, and then looks away. Embarrassed, I close my eyes and say nothing.

From deep in the shadows, I hear the heavy, wooden door of the hammam open, then close. Soon, from another of the rooms, I hear the low, steady intonations of a man praying, chanting, his husky voice drifting through the darkness. Abruptly, he stops, and the silence is followed by the sound of water pouring into a metal bucket, then splashing, then pouring, then splashing, then pouring—followed again by the soft, hypnotic rhythm of prayer.

I look up and notice that Abayomi is gone.

'Abayomi,' I say, leaning forward, peering into the darkness, 'are you still—?'

I become silent.

My hand against the wall, I rise and walk slowly through the heavy, hot clouds of steam from one chamber of the hammam to the next.

Stepping into the chamber nearest the hammam's entrance, I stop.

Far in the corner, nearly hidden within the clouds of steam, I see Abayomi. He is turned away from me, his silver hair and dark shoulders eerily aglow beneath the dull light on the wall above him.

'Abayomi,' I whisper, 'it's me, Ulysses. I'm leaving now.'

Slowly, he looks over his shoulder at me. Saying nothing, he again turns away, bending forward into the darkness.

I move closer toward him. He is no longer wearing a towel, I notice; his thin, bare ass moves slowly back and forth.

'Abayomi,' I say, 'what are—what are you—?'

I fall silent and watch, terrified, as he stands straight and, stepping back, turns toward me. My mouth open but unable to speak, I can only stand, staring.

'Now you,' he says, smiling.

In the corner, pushed up against the stone wall, I see a young, dark-skinned boy, no older than twelve. He turns, looking at me, and then, as if underwater, falls to the floor; he does not make a sound.

I feel a hand lightly touch my shoulder. I quickly turn, startled. It is Abayomi.

'But,' I begin to say, 'you were—'

I move away from him, looking into the heavy, shadowed clouds of steam. The young boy is gone and the room is empty, silent.

'Son,' I hear Abayomi say.

I turn, looking at his dark, sad face.

'Son,' he asks, 'why are you crying?'

He extends his arms, as if to catch me. I open my mouth and begin to fall. I keep falling.

'It all comes together in the end,' he says. 'And sometimes not even then. We look back, and what do we remember? I have two memories from the first ten years of my life. That's it. A decade of living, and, out of it all, I remember two things: eating biscuits and cracklings with my father and finding a turquoise ring by the side of the road.

'My mother died when I was three, but I don't remember that. I had part of my ear bit off by a horse, but I don't remember that, either. Just two more things I was told about later in life but that I don't personally recall.

'So, it's not even like I remember what was important and forget what wasn't—or even like I block out the bad memories and remember the good. For whatever reason, and who knows what it is, this or that particular moment gets stuck in my brain, but most of it doesn't. Just pictures. That's all it comes down to: a few pictures here and there in our mind that come together to form a life, our life.

'The real truth, though, the *reality* of our lives, well, I won't even guess where that lives. Maybe it just disappears. Do you think? Just crumbles away like—like a charred piece of paper. Or, worse, like it was never even real to begin with. Like, who knows, maybe it was just something we imagined along the way. Do you think?'

She kisses my eyelids, then my mouth; her lips are cool, dry.

'Maggie,' I begin to say, 'it's—'

'Be quiet,' she interrupts.

I open my eyes, look at her, and then close them again.

'Love, Ulysses,' I hear her whisper. 'It's about love.'

'Trust nothing, no one. Love is vanity turned outward. Pride is shame in search of redemption; art is pride is love is shit. Religion is moot.'

His finger touches my lips.

'Silence,' he says. 'We must now have silence.'

Maggie sits on the bed next to mine, smiling. She is dressed entirely in white: long skirt, blouse, scarf, shoes. Removing the scarf from her hair and her shoulders, she folds it and sets it in her lap.

Dangling from her ears, I notice, are tiny silver and topaz earrings, oval-shaped.

'Hey, sleeping beauty,' she says, 'did my kisses wake you?'

I say nothing, looking at her.

'Are you awake yet?' she asks, reaching over and gently touching my bare shoulder.

On the right side of her neck, where her earlobe meets her jawbone, is a small, round sore.

'What happened?' I ask.

'When?' she replies, as if confused.

'To your neck.'

'Oh, that,' she says, quickly, gently touching her neck. 'That's nothing. I burnt myself with a cigarette. Hey, did you miss me?'

'Don't change the subject,' I reply, sitting straight.

'Change the subject? I wasn't. You asked me what happened and I told you. Ulysses, are you in—'

She looks at me, suddenly apprehensive.

'Are you in a bad mood?' she continues. 'Because if you are, then I'd just as soon leave.'

'I'm not in a bad mood,' I reply, raising my hands and stretching.

'Are you sure about that?' she asks.

'I said so, didn't I?'

She watches me.

'I saw YaYa downstairs,' she says. 'He said he hadn't seen you since the night I left, that every time he came by you were sleeping.'

'I was tired.'

'Forty hours of sleep,' she says. 'I guess you were tired.'

'Forty hours? What? Was he timing me?'

'No, but he said he remembered when you went to bed, and it was over forty hours ago. You went to the hammam, came back, and went to bed.'

'Well,' I reply, resting against the headboard and putting my hands in my lap, 'if he had done a better job of spying on me, he would know I wasn't asleep the entire time.'

She looks at me, frowning, then says:

'You know what, Ulysses? I'm going to go now. When you're in a better mood, you can come look for me.'

Taking the scarf from her lap, she drapes it around her shoulders and picks up her purse. I am silent, watching her.

'We're not married, you know,' she says.

I say nothing.

'I'm not your husband,' she continues, 'and you're not my wife. And unless I'm mistaken, neither are you a cat on a hot tin roof, Ulysses.'

'What's that supposed to mean?' I ask, looking at the sore on her neck.

'What it means,' she replies, 'is that you're acting like the worst stereotype of a jealous woman, which in reality is just a jealous man.'

'Who said I was jealous?' I ask. 'Besides, what do I have to be jealous of?'

'Nothing,' she says. 'But what does anybody have to be jealous of?'

'Whatever,' I reply, shrugging.

She looks at me for a moment, then stands and walks silently out of the room, shutting the door behind her.

Later that evening, I walk downstairs to the café; Maggie and YaYa are seated at a table across from one another, talking. Seeing me, they abruptly become silent. YaYa waves, while Maggie turns away and lights a cigarette.

'Have a seat, stranger,' YaYa says.

'What were you guys whispering about?' I ask, sitting down between them.

'What is wrong with you?' Maggie asks, turning angrily at me. 'We weren't whispering; we were talking.'

'Okay,' I reply, shrugging my shoulders. 'If you say so.'

'Actually,' she says, looking at YaYa, 'we were whispering because we didn't want anyone to hear us plotting our crimes. Right, YaYa?'

'Hey, don't bring me into this,' YaYa replies, laughing, holding up his hands as if to surrender. 'I'm just an innocent bystander.'

'Ignorance is not innocence but sin,' I say, looking not at YaYa but at Maggie.

'Is this another one of your father's maxims?' Maggie asks, her eyes ablaze. 'Or would it be your grandfather's?'

'Elizabeth Barrett Browning,' I reply. '1806 to 1861.'

'How educated of you,' she snaps.

'I think I'll go take a walk,' YaYa says, closing his notebook and setting it atop the yellow pad of legal paper.

'YaYa,' I say, closing my eyes and shaking my head, 'stay. Please. I'm just being an asshole.'

'You can say that again,' Maggie says, taking a drag of her cigarette.

'I'm just being an asshole,' I repeat, looking at the sore on her neck. She looks away.

'Actually,' YaYa says, standing, 'I was just about to head up to my room anyway. But I'll check you guys out when I come back down. Okay?'

'You sure?' I ask, looking up at him.

'Positive,' he says, squeezing my shoulder and picking up his belongings.

He slides his chair beneath the table and looks at us.

'Both of you,' he says, 'chill.'

He turns and leaves; Maggie and I look at one another.

'See,' she says, 'you've made him cry.'

'He'll get over it,' I reply. 'I'm sure.'

She stares at me and says:

'You're acting like an idiot, Ulysses.'

'I know.'

She shakes her head.

'What's wrong with you?' she asks. 'Did you have yet another nervous breakdown?'

I look at her.

'Is that a joke?' I ask.

'No,' she replies, 'it isn't. Because either you're a very jealous, moody person or—or you're having a nervous breakdown. And considering I've only ever seen you in one mood, regardless of the situation, it must mean you're—'

'And what is that one mood?' I ask, interrupting her.

'Your one mood is—is *no* mood. You call it smooth; I call it emotionless. Angry, happy, tired, whatever—one mood. No mood. And don't get me wrong, sweetheart; I like a man under control. But when things start to slip, it makes me wonder if he was ever really in control or just good at hiding his true self all along.'

I stare at the small round sore on her neck.

'I return from two days with Jonathan,' she continues, 'and, bam, you act like—like I'm your wife and I've just returned from the arms of my lover.'

The two men at the table next to ours, I notice, are watching us. I wave my hand and they turn away.

'You're imagining things,' I say.

'No,' she replies, 'I'm not.'

'Yes,' I say, 'you are. Have I ever said anything about Jonathan? Have I ever, the few times I've seen him, been rude to him? Or in any way acted jealous?'

'No, you haven't. But so what? You're like every other man; you confuse saying nothing with feeling nothing. And it doesn't work that way, Ulysses. It comes out in the end. All of it.'

'What comes out?'

'Everything stuck inside of you.'

'All I wanted to know,' I say, looking at her, 'is how you got that sore on your neck. That's what I want to know.'

She looks at me, disgusted, then stands.

'I was wrong,' she says. 'You're not crazy; you're pathetic. And I can deal with any kind of man but a man I pity.'

Taking her purse, she quickly turns and leaves, rushing through the tables and out onto the street. I rummage through my pocket, toss some money onto the table, and chase after her.

Turning into the plaza, she begins to run, her long, white scarf fluttering behind her. Across the plaza and through the Medina's entrance, she disappears into the darkness outside the high, stone walls.

I follow.

Catching up to her as she nears the beach, I grab hold of her arm. She pulls away and stops, glaring at me. Even in the darkness, I can see that she is furious.

'When most women run,' she says, stepping away from me, 'they want to be followed—but not me, brother. Now fuck off!'

I stand and watch silently as she turns and walks through the darkness toward the beach. As I watch, I ask myself if I should return to the hotel or follow her.

'Follow her,' I whisper.

I continue behind her, but more slowly now, trailing her by perhaps ten feet. She continues walking, ignoring my presence.

Abruptly, she stops and, not turning around, says:

'Ulysses, please, just go away.'

I walk up to her and place my hand on her shoulder. Suddenly, she spins around and slaps me across the face with one hand, then the other.

'Didn't you hear me?' she screams. 'Go away. Leave me alone. Fuck off. Get lost.'

'Maggie—' I begin to say.

'Oh fuck!' she screams. 'You are turning a—a minor incident into something very ugly, Ulysses. Why don't you just leave before it gets any uglier? Please.'

Her shoulders slump, as if in defeat, and frowning sadly, she whispers:

'Please.'

'What happened to your neck?' I ask. 'Tell me that and I'll leave.'

Suddenly, she begins to laugh.

'What happened to my neck?' she says, still laughing. 'Listen to you. Just listen to you. What the hell do you *think* happened to my neck? What?'

'I think you burnt yourself,' I reply.

'I told you I burnt myself,' she says, no longer laughing.

'I think you did it on purpose.'

'And? So what if I did?'

'Did you? Or did Jonathan?'

'Jonathan? What makes you think he would—?'

She stares at me silently. A look of terror passes across her face like a blush.

'Let me ask you something,' she says.

I am silent. I watch her.

'Would you rather have a father who never said he loved you,' she asks, 'or one who crept into your room every night and fucked you?'

I raise my hand, putting it against her warm cheek.

'Answer me,' she says, pulling away.

I shake my head.

'Love,' I say. 'You said it was about love.'

Parking my truck in the driveway, I turn off the ignition and open the door. As I step out of the truck, I turn and look at my luggage on the seat. I'll come back for it later, I think. Slamming the door behind me, I walk slowly toward the house.

It is a warm, sunny late-afternoon; the only sound is of the soft wind rustling through the leaves. Stepping up onto the porch, I stop and look into the trees that separate the yard from the river. It is as if I never left.

Opening the door, I step inside. It is warm and dark, quiet. The curtains above the sink are drawn. On the table is a coffee cup. Standing near the door, I look around, then turn and walk upstairs.

In my bedroom, I sit on the edge of the bed and look at the rows of books, then out the window. I think briefly of Maggie; immediately, the thought vanishes.

I leave the room and walk slowly down the hallway to my father's room. The door is closed; I look for a moment at the faded, peeling red paint.

'Is that you, Ulysses?' I hear my father call.

Opening the door, I look into the room; he is lying in his bed, the sheet pulled up to his chest, staring at me.

'Who else would it be?' I reply.
'Where have you been?' he asks.
'Out,' I answer.
'Well,' he says, 'you could've told me you were leaving. I saw your truck was gone and—well, you could've told me.'
'I'm sorry,' I say. 'I should've told you. I know. But I'm back now. Do you need anything?'
'No,' he says, 'I can take care of myself, thank you.'
'Alright, alright,' I reply. 'I was just asking.'
I look at him for a moment, then say:
'Well, if you do need anything, just call me. I'll be downstairs.'
He nods his head.
'Do you want the door shut?' I ask. 'Or opened?'
'It was closed before you opened it,' he answers.
Shaking my head, I turn, shut the door, and go downstairs.

'It was never about love,' she says, taking my hand from her face. 'It was about the loss of love. There's a difference, Ulysses.'
Letting go of my hand, she turns and walks slowly toward the rolling ebb and tide of the ocean. I do not follow.

'Didn't you hear me?' he asks.
I look up from the stack of pictures on my desk. He is standing in the doorway, staring angrily at me.
'I'm sorry, Dad,' I say, setting a picture atop the pile. 'Were you calling me?'
'Why are you talking like that?' he asks, looking at me as if I have spoken in a language other than English.
'Like what?' I ask.
'Like *that!*'
'And how is *that?*' I reply, irritated.
'So slowly,' he answers.
'Dad,' I say, 'what can I do for you? I'm not in the mood to—'

'You told me,' he says, interrupting me, 'to call you if I needed anything.'

'Okay,' I say. 'What do you need?'

'Why do you keep looking at those pictures?' he asks.

'Is that what you needed? To ask me why I'm talking so—so slowly and why I'm looking at these pictures? And I don't *keep* looking at them.'

'Yes, you do. And it's pathetic.'

'Dad,' I say, 'unless you actually need anything, why don't you—'

'Every chance you get,' he interrupts, 'you sit there looking at those old pictures like they were—that was a long time ago, boy.'

I peer down at the picture of Maggie; she is smiling, dressed in red, smoking a cigarette. In the left hand corner of the photograph, I see Jonathan's arm and hand resting on the cluttered café table.

'So what?' I say, looking up at my father. 'A long time ago is sometimes just around the corner. You should know that, if anyone should.'

'What do you mean by that?' he asks. 'And stop talking like that, damnit.'

I look around the room, at the floor, the walls, the ceiling. I look at the rows of books, out the window, and again at my father. When, I wonder, did he get so old? Though still big and broad, he now has the posture and gait of a crippled workhorse.

Like my grandfather, I think.

'Bullshit,' I say. 'All of it, bullshit.'

He looks at me, silent.

'Sound familiar?' I ask.

Still he says nothing.

'Everything was bullshit to him,' I say. 'Even you—and me.'

I watch him standing in the doorway, and I remember when he was young, younger—when we both were.

'Why didn't you do anything, Dad?' I ask.

He stares at me, then turns to leave.

'I'm talking to you,' I say.

He disappears silently around the corner.

'Dad,' I yell, jumping up and walking after him, 'I'm talking to you!'

I follow him into his bedroom. He sits on the edge of the bed and stares down at the floor. Standing in the doorway, I look at him.

'Why didn't you do anything?' I ask again.

'I don't know what you're talking about,' he replies.

'Oh, yes you do, old man,' I say. 'You know damned well what I'm talking about—about the past being right around the corner.'

I speak slowly, without emotion. I am empty.

'Now answer my question!' I demand. 'Why didn't you do anything?'

'I don't know what you're talking about,' he repeats, still looking at the floor.

'Yes, you do.'

'No, I don't.'

'Oh, really?' I say. 'Well, then, let me remind you, Dad.'

'No!' he suddenly yells, looking up at me. His voice is deep and loud, and briefly I am a boy again, frightened.

Still I continue:

'From the time I was seven—'

'No!' he yells.

'Until I was thirteen—'

'Liar!'

'Your father, my grandfather.'

'Liar!'

'Night after night—'

'No,' he whispers.

'Came into my room, not even bothering to shut the door behind him—'

'No.'

'And—'

He is silent now.

'Telling me,' I continue, 'that it wouldn't hurt as much if I took a deep breath. Telling me he—'

Though I cannot hear him, I can see his mouth move.

'Telling me,' I continue, 'I was lucky his dick was so small. Did you ever see his dick? It was the smallest thing, Dad. It hurt, but it was—'

I stop.

'And you knew,' I say.

Silence.

'And you knew,' I repeat.

'That's a lie,' he says, softly.

'You knew,' I say, ignoring him, 'and you didn't stop it. Why?'

'That's a goddamned lie,' he says, looking at me.

I walk to the bed, standing above him.

If I were to kill you, I think, it would not be because of this.

'There is no way you could've lived in this house all those years,' I say, 'and not known what was happening.'

'It's a lie. You're lying.'

There is a moment of complete silence.

'No,' I say, 'I'm not.'

Slowly but roughly, I grab my father by his shoulders and push him back against the bed. Simply, quietly, he lies there, looking up at me.

'Why?' I ask, bending over him, my hands pinning his shoulders to the bed. 'I want you to tell me why.'

Passive, emotionless, he looks into my eyes and says:

'I don't know what you're—'

Before he can finish, I move forward, up, rising onto the bed. With one knee on his chest, the other at his side, I put my hands around his neck. He begins to resist, but soon stops.

It is, I will later think, as if he wanted to die.

He dies quickly.

I relax my grip, and he coughs once. A fleck of blood lands on his upper cheek. I tighten my grip. Soon his dead eyes stare up at me, and still I strangle.

Letting go, I turn, then step onto the floor, staring at him. His hands are at his side, his feet resting on the floor. One of his slippers, I notice, has fallen off.

'The thing about taking ourselves so seriously,' I whisper, looking at him, 'is that so many before us have done it better.'

I step forward and, lifting his legs, pull him up onto the bed, slowly, deliberately. Propping his head on the pillow as if he is merely asleep, I begin to undress him. I do not know why.

When he is naked, I fold his clothes and put them in the top drawer of his dresser. I take a dark red blanket and put it across his feet. I turn, walking slowly downstairs and out of the house. I go to the barn, find the shovel, and walk into the woods near the house.

In one box, I place his head. In the next, I place his left arm. Like Pandora, in reverse, I place each piece in a separate wooden box, then nail it shut. It is my gift, I think, God's gift, everything where it belongs, hidden, stored. I will take these seven boxes, and I will bury them. Head, right arm, left arm, right leg, left leg, torso, and privates.

'Privates,' I whisper, smiling, as I nail the final box shut. 'Not so private, old man, huh?'

Stacking the boxes, one on top of the other, I stand back and look at them. In each, I think, is a bit of ugliness, a bit of pain: seven wooden boxes that together make a man, the memory of a man; a *father*.

Turning, I face the darkness behind me. Like a curtain, the darkness slowly pulls itself in a circle around me until, finally, I am lost, alone, within it.

Stepping forward, I raise my hands and shuffle hesitantly through the blackness.

'Ye are of your father, the devil,' I hear a voice whisper.

I stop.

'And the lusts of your father, ye will do,' the voice continues. 'He was a murderer from the beginning and abode not in the truth, because there is no truth in him. When he speaketh a lie, he speaketh of his own: for he is a liar and the father of it.'

I turn and walk slowly to the end of the hallway. If I think of anything, it is of the need to think nothing, aware of only that which is before me: the dark red walls, the wooden floor, my movement past, upon.

My grandfather's bedroom door is open. Passing, I glance inside the small, windowless room, but I do not stop.

At the end of the hallway, I stand before my father's bedroom and slowly open the door. He is on the bed beneath the window, his naked body stretched out in the dim, early-evening light. The room is warm and small, shadow overlapping shadow, with a bed, dresser, and desk. I step through the narrow doorway and walk to the bed.

His hands are at his side, legs together, his face tilted up and to the left as if, upon death, he had been looking out the window. His eyes are closed, as is his mouth, and on his left cheek, just below the eye, is a single drop of blood. I look up at the ceiling, then down. Across his feet is a dark red blanket.

His body is nearly hairless. He is a big man, tall and broad, muscular, with huge, worn hands and feet. Like me, he is uncircumcised. His cock is big, I think, but his balls are small, like a young boy's or a bodybuilder's, and briefly I am embarrassed. I raise my head and look out the window into the clear, dark sky.

I close my eyes, whispering:

'You can think of a whole lot of good stuff to tell a nigger when you're—'

I open my eyes and reach for the edge of the dull gray bed sheet on which he lies. I pull it up and over him, then walk around to the opposite side of the bed and do the same. I wrap him with the thin sheet, as if in a cocoon, and then knot its ends. I do this as if I have done it before.

I move quickly and lift him up, over my shoulder, holding his legs with both of my arms. Staring down at the wooden floor, I step forward and say:

'One.'

Though not as heavy as I had imagined, his limbs are stiff, awkward, and I stumble with the body out of the room, down the narrow stairway, through the kitchen, and out of the house.

'Thirty-one, thirty-two,' I whisper, 'thirty-three, thirty-four, thirty-five.'

I move slowly across the yard and through the trees, staring at the ground as I walk.

'Fifty-two, fifty-three, fifty-four.'

The path through the trees is narrow and sloping, winding. I move with caution.

'Eighty-nine, ninety, ninety-one, ninety-two.'

Reaching the empty grave, I take a final step.

'One hundred and seventeen.'

Kneeling, I lean forward, then lie the body by the side of the grave. I stand. Breathing deeply, slowly, I rest my hands on my hips and look around.

From deep in the shadows that rise up around the small clearing, I hear the quick, lone hoot of an owl. Above me, the sky is clear and dark, darkening. I am tempted, briefly, to return to the house for a lantern. I do not.

I kneel again, take the end of the sheet, and slowly, carefully, lower my father into his grave. Satisfied with the body's position, I stand, grab the shovel, and begin to fill the shallow grave with dirt. I move quickly, thoughtlessly.

I work nonstop until I am done. I am done sooner than I had expected. An hour, two hours, three? Twenty minutes? I do not know.

I drop the shovel at my side and look into the darkness. I am sweating, trembling. Across my back, from shoulder to shoulder, is a sharp pain. My left hand, between the thumb and forefinger, is raw, bleeding.

Like a door opening, then abruptly closing, a thought begins to form and, just as quickly, fade. Staring into the trees, I whisper:

'She belonged to you. Watch.'

Turning, I step away from the grave and walk through the trees to the river. I take off my boots and undress. I fold my clothes and place them neatly in a pile next to my boots.

Naked, I step slowly into the cool, black, slow-flowing water and swim to its center. A breeze flutters across the surface, causing me to shiver as I look up into the night, close my eyes, and let myself sink.

Feeling the soft, cold muck of the riverbed with my feet and hands, I rest, motionless, then push myself up out of the water, blinking, and look into the warm, dark night. Above me, like a round window, the moon glows, shining, its soft, blue light illuminating the shadows beneath, between, the darkness.

'You can stop now,' I whisper.

Paddling to the river's bank, I step from the water and, still naked, return to the house. Shutting and locking the door behind me, I move into the kitchen. I sit at the table, listening, looking. Everything is quiet. I could die here, I think, looking into the shadows. So quiet, as quiet as—here, now, in my father's house. So still, so quiet. Closing my eyes, I smile.

Also from Akashic Books

The Snow Train by Joseph Cummins
290 pages, trade paperback, ISBN: 1-888451-23-8
AKB17 - $14.95

"A groundbreaking first novel that tackles nothing less daunting than the fragile psyche of early childhood."
–Kaylie Jones, author of *A Soldier's Daughter Never Cries*
"An intriguing worldview, meticulously assembled with an artist's inspired touch." –*Kirkus Reviews*

Heart of the Old Country by Tim McLoughlin
*Selected for the Barnes & Noble
Discover Great New Writers Program*
216 pages, trade paperback, ISBN: 1-888451-15-7
AKB11 - $14.95

"Tim McLoughlin writes about South Brooklyn with a fidelity to people and place reminiscent of James T. Farrell's *Studs Lonigan* and George Orwell's *Down and Out in Paris and London* . . . No voice in this symphony of a novel is more impressive than that of Mr. McLoughlin, a young writer with a rare gift for realism and empathy."
—Sidney Offit, author of *Memoir of the Bookie's Son*

Water in Darkness by Daniel Buckman
193 pages, hardcover, ISBN: 1-888451-19-X
AKB13 - $21.00

"Simply put, *Water in Darkness* is a superb novel . . . an earthbound 'Chicago' style that harkens back to *Studs Lonigan*, and reminds one of the close-to-the-bone, walk-the-plank stories of Mike Royko, Stuart Dybek, and Nelson Algren. Buckman speaks for a new, young generation of soldiers who thought they were at peace . . . the best new fiction I have read in a good long while."
—Larry Heinemann, author of *Paco's Story*, winner of the National Book Award

Adios Muchachos by Daniel Chavarría
Nominated for a 2001 Edgar Award!
245 pages, paperback, ISBN: 1-888451-16-5
AKB12 - $13.95

A selection in the Akashic Cuban Noir series.
"...[A] zesty Cuban paella of a novel that's impossible to put down. This is a great read..." –*Library Journal*

Jerusalem Calling by Joel Schalit
218 pages, trade paperback, ISBN: 1-888451-17-3
AKB20 - $14.95

"This remarkable collection of essays by an astute young writer covers a wide range of topics–the political ethic of punk, the nature of secular Jewish identity, the dangerous place, according to Schalit, that politicized Christianity plays in the U.S., and the legacy of the Cold War in the ability to imagine freedom. Schalit almost always hits his mark... This is the debut of a new and original thinker." –*Publishers Weekly* (starred review)

Spy's Fate by Arnaldo Correa
305 pages, hardcover, ISBN: 1-888451-28-9
AKB26 - $24.95

"Arnaldo Correa gives us a courageous book that offers a true insider's view of the new Cuba: the Cuba that has emerged since the fall of the Soviet Union; the Cuba that neither the United States government nor Fidel Castro wants you to know about."

–William Heffernan,
Edgar Award-winning author of *Red Angel*

These books are available at local bookstores.
They can also be purchased with a credit card online through www.akashicbooks.com.

To order by mail, send a check or money order to:
Akashic Books
PO Box 1456
New York, NY 10009

Prices include shipping.
Outside the U.S., add $3 to each book ordered.

Born November 18, 1967 to a horse-trainer and an artist, **Mustafa Mutabaruka** currently lives in New York City.